THE WITC

The witch and her dog have guarded the cave for centuries. But Dave and Maddy are the only ones to guess that she is more than stone, that there really is a sad old woman behind the stories. Even so, they are amazed when the witch starts demanding food and clothes to keep her warm.

The recent death of their own grand-mother inspires the children to take pity on old Hester Wookey. Soon, however, her eccentric and ungrateful behaviour makes them wish they hadn't…

Beth Webb lives in Somerset with her four children and an entourage of pets. Her stories are mostly based on real places or events, intertwined with traditional folk legends. This, she says, is a good excuse for going out somewhere nice for the day and taking a book of old tales to read.

Beth Webb's other children's books for Lion Publishing are *The Magic in the Pool of Making*, *The Dragons of Kilve*, *Fleabag and the Ring Fire*, *Fleabag and the Fire Cat* and *Foxdown Wood*.

To my son John Ralls

To Francesca

The Witch of Wookey Hole

best wishes

Beth Webb

Beth Webb.

A LION BOOK

Published by
Lion Publishing plc
Sandy Lane West, Oxford, England
ISBN 0 7459 3894 9

First edition 1998
10 9 8 7 6 5 4 3 2 1

A catalogue record for this book is available
from the British Library

Typeset in 11.25/13 Garamond
Printed and bound in Great Britain
by Caledonian International Book
Manufacturing, Glasgow

Acknowledgments
In loving memory of Marcelina, who always had a
twinkle and a smile.
  I am grateful to the staff of Wookey Hole caves,
especially the guides who have answered my endless
questions with unflagging helpfulness and enthusiasm.
Also to Sue Lord and Gerard Stewart, without whose
help and support this book would probably never
have happened.
  Thank you to the Somerset Fire Brigade for their
advice.
  Special thanks are also due to Maddy, Gabs and John
for their helpful interest. Maddy, thank you for lending
me your name!

Contents

Someone
Unpleasant

1

The little green light of the witch danced across the cave walls, then it was gone.

Dave froze. He found himself grabbing at his sister's sleeve. For the first time ever, she didn't tug away in disgust. *She* could feel something frightening too, he was certain.

It wasn't the silly green light that scared them. Anyone could see *that* was a trick with the guide's torch.

No. It was more than that.

'There's someone here!' Dave whispered.

Maddy hesitated and swallowed hard before tugging her arm back. 'Of course, you dope! *We're* here. The whole class…'

Dave shoved his hands deep into his pockets and hung his head, feeling his cheeks burning. It wasn't just them, and Maddy knew it. There was someone else here, someone from hundreds of lonely years ago. Dave shivered. A grey, cool dampness hung with an unhappy ache all around. It was such a sad, hurting sort of place. A horrid, prickly sensation slithered up and down his spine. He wanted to run away and hide.

But he couldn't. They were on a tour. There was nowhere to run off to, anyway. He glanced around. The twisting rocky chamber was piled with boulders all along the right-hand side. He might be able to dash up there and wait until the others all came past again on the way out…

But what if they didn't come back that way? He would be left alone, in the dark.

With *the presence*.

Maddy raised an eyebrow in his direction. She could see he was really scared. She felt a little sorry for him. Dave could always feel things, all sorts of things. He was often right too. He'd been right about Gran feeling cold and alone. She had wished she had listened to him then. After Gran died, Maddy had secretly promised herself she'd always at least listen to what Dave had to say in future…

'What's bugging you?' she whispered, although in her heart of hearts she already knew.

Not far away, someone unpleasant was waiting. Someone who did not *want* an endless stream of visitors ogling and giggling in her home, day after day. And what was worse, this mysterious 'someone' was still there. Old and rheumaticky, the Witch of Wookey Hole was watching them, coughing and spitting at the endless tourists!

Before Dave had a chance to speak, the twins became separated as the other children jostled and fought for the best positions to see the curious shapes in the rocks.

Standing above them on the pile of fallen boulders, the young guide was relishing the squeals of horror from his audience as he embroidered his story a little

8

more and sent the bright green witch-light dancing across the rock-face once again.

But Maddy and Dave were not even listening.

For a split second, they could both *see* the cave as it had been all those centuries ago when a lonely old woman was still living there, huddled under smelly, half-cured sheepskins strewn over the limestone slabs to make some sort of a bed. Behind her hung a rickety old hand loom strung with rough, grey wool and stretched by knobby clay weights. Next to her a greasy stew was cooking in a rusty iron pot over a smouldering fire. A big black dog was there too, gnawing at a bone… and somewhere nearby there was a goat bleating.

The old woman looked very miserable and cold.

Suddenly Big Henry, the class bully, clattered past and jerked the twins out of their reverie. Dave and Maddy were always his favourite targets. The class was on the move, pushing, shoving, chattering and squealing as twenty-four pairs of well-shod feet shuffled down the stone steps to the next chamber, everyone following the thin young man in the green overalls.

At the bottom of the slimy stairs the passage narrowed between a display of stalactites on the left and a stone parapet on the right. Dave was so busy staring around he did not watch where he was going and slipped, ending up with his backside in a wet puddle. But then *he* would! Maddy looked down at her brother and tutted. 'Typical!' she sniffed and yanked under his armpit to get him up. He was cold and shaking.

Secretly, Maddy felt sorry for him. She wasn't surprised he had slipped. He must be even more scared

9

than she was… this place was enough to make anyone lose their footing. There was so much anger and loneliness down here.

'I *heard* her Mad…' he started to whisper urgently. 'I heard her crying!' But their teacher glowered at him to be quiet and listen to the guide.

'And the people of Wookey Hole village were so frightened by the witch and her terrible spells that they sent all the way to Glastonbury, which was a long way in those days…' The thin young man was talking again. 'And they fetched one of them Glastonbury monks to come and sort her out—and sort her out he did. He got straight on his old donkey and came along to Wookey with a bell, book and candle in his pocket. And he challenged the old girl in the chamber we've just come from, right in her front room, you might say. And he said, "You oughtn't to be putting curses on godly folk, that you shouldn't!"

'But the old witch lady didn't give a fig for the monk, that she didn't! She just jumped on her broomstick and flew all the way down to this chamber here, the witch's kitchen, where local people believed that hell began.'

At the touch of a switch, the guide turned on a flickering crimson light that made the rocks look as if they were on fire. By the eerie red glow, the children could see a large chamber, bigger than a cathedral, with strange-shaped stalactites and stalagmites on the left, and a huge, green, icy-looking lake to their right.

Dave tugged at Maddy's anorak. 'It's not hell, it's just lonely.'

'I suppose it could be the same thing,' muttered his sister.

Then the lights were turned off again, so it was completely dark. 'Imagine you had just a candle down here...' the guide whispered softly and eerily.

Twenty-four children groaned and shivered.

'Then the good monk caught up with the witch, right where you're standing.'

At this, the children jumped back and squealed in terrified delight.

'Then he made the sign of the cross, which turned the whole lake into holy water, just like that! Then the monk scooped up a whole bucketful of water and he doused her with it, good and proper. Then with a terrible scream, a blinding flash of light and a crack of thunder, the witch was turned to stone—and that's how she's stayed to this very day!'

The guide pressed another switch and floodlit a knobbly shape to their right. Suddenly the lumpy stalagmite became a looming profile of what might have been a large head with an old-fashioned bonnet, leaning sadly out over the water. Crouching behind her in the shadows was a small, lumpy stone which could have been a sleeping dog.

Some children gasped, others giggled.

'I wonder what her name was?' Maddy whispered to Dave. He just shrugged. He'd been going to say something oafish like 'Old Mother Hubbard,' but somehow it stuck in his throat. Whoever she was, she had had enough. She did not need any more jokes made about her.

Still as 2 Stone

Hester Wookey had stayed very still for a very long time.

So long, in fact, that she had no idea whether she could still move or not. She had always been stiff in the joints and all her potions had done little to ease the pain. She was so stiff she had even given up dancing. But that was a long time ago… long before that meddling monk had come with all his hocus-pocus nonsense. He had seemed kindly enough at first—then he started threatening to turn her to stone!' How dare he! But the more he waved his arms around and muttered his strange Latin words, the more the terrified old lady thought that *stone* might not be a bad idea.

So as the monk waved his arms in the air and splashed holy water around, she sat down firmly on the nearest rock and stayed stock-still to make everyone think she really *had* turned to stone.

It had been hard to keep up, but it had worked. Despite the terrible cramps in her arms and legs and the cold in her bottom, she had managed it. Everyone had gone away. But she had been so frightened by all the lights and noise and fuss that, despite the discomfort, she stayed quite still even after her accusers had gone. It was hard, but she had made herself do it. The men might have left watchers to catch her if she moved. Who knew what spies might have been left behind lurking in the blackness…?

Then, in the endless, fearful darkness, the naiads—water people—had come to her with their songs and their soothing touch. Hester had never been quite sure *what* they were singing, but it made her feel very calm and still inside. She had soon found that she did not need to try and stay still, she *was* still. All over!

And it was a good job too, for then more terrible men had come with their exploding sticks to shoot down the stalactites—those graceful, hanging needles of stone which had been such a beautiful part of her home. Her only beauty, in fact. Then there had been the silly dinner parties and morris dancers banging their sticks and stamping their feet, although she had liked the bells and the music… Oh, and then there had been the witch-hunting expeditions—she had stayed quite still for them as well.

But when all the noise and fuss was gone and everything was quiet, she liked to listen to the gentle sound of the eternal dripping. That was soothing and good. It made her feel as if *something* bothered to stop and talk to her. The water was her friend, her lullaby. Sometimes, when no one had come by for years (she couldn't tell how long in the cool, calm darkness) the streams and drips sang restful songs and she found a sort of contentment. Sometimes the singing almost had words, and she wondered whether the naiads had come back. But all the sounds melted into each other in the cool, dark caves. She could never be really sure.

She didn't need to move in these quiet times. Stillness and the soft sounds of water went together.

Then the men had come with drills and made strange kinds of lights that made no smoke and never burned low. The effects were quite pretty. She liked watching the colours flickering and sparkling on the water below. She stayed still for that too. She had never seen her magnificent home so cleverly lit. It was much grander than even she had imagined. Then other men had come with the wet, sticky stuff that turned into something hard like rock and made walkways.

Still she did not move, for fear the pretty lights might be taken away, and she would be left on her own in the dark again.

What she did *not* like were the endless people who tramped past almost every day and heard the wicked and libellous stories about how she was supposed to have been an evil witch! As if she would—or even could—have given a plague of boils to the villagers, or made their goats drop dead.

She was too frightened of everyone to have done anything like that. She'd *thought* of it, true, but she would not have dreamed of ever really hurting anyone.

Anyway, all these years sitting on her own in her cave had been to escape from horrid lies like those. All that time she had not so much as blinked. She was terrified that if people realized she was still there, they would come and chase her with dogs like they had so many times before.

One night, when all the noise and people were gone, she made up her mind. The time had come for her to move. She was going to get up from this cold old rock and go deeper into the caves. Somewhere they would never find her. Somewhere she could be alone and untroubled for ever.

She tried to stretch out her hands to ease herself up… but she could *not* move!

What Hester did not know was that the naiads' songs of rock and water had actually turned her to stone. Then the kindly water people had disguised the old lady by moulding cool mud and water down her face and back, leaving streaks of calcium carbonate over every limb, making her look gnarled and knobbly. Just like an ancient stalagmite. No one would tell there had ever *really* been an old lady there. Hester had not noticed any of this. She thought the naiads' careful work was the ordinary water that always dripped from the roof of the cave.

She also did not know the naiads' songs had been well meant, hiding her from unkind persecutors. The water people and the monk had talked together, and decided that making the old lady seem to turn to stone would be the best thing they could do for her, protecting her from the mean-minded people outside.

Hester had only heard the songs, and felt the coolness of the water. It had been soothing then, but now she wanted to move again she felt panic spreading through her rigid body. Terrified, she tried with supreme efforts to wrench herself free, to twist her unyielding bones… To call out to someone—*anyone*!

The creaking and cracking noise of the old lady's movements brought geologists by the dozen to ascertain whether the caves were still safe for the public. Hester was surrounded night and day with electronic instruments and analysts of every kind. It was not safe for the water people to get near to Hester and undo their work. So the poor old lady was left locked in her stony cage, alone, cold and very frightened.

Despite the geologists swarming everywhere, no one could find anything wrong. Seismologists set up their equipment and poked around for days. But they had no luck either, and still the creaking continued as Hester struggled to free herself.

Day after day she cried, but drips of clear, cool water were always falling from the vast limestone roof above. A few more running down the face of the stone witch were not noticed by anyone. And worst of all, any attempt to move hurt terribly. It could have been the thick limescale deposits pulling at her skin but all her joints and every muscle had turned to stone as well. How she ached! How cold she was! How terribly alone!

At last the experts went away, baffled.

The next day, a party of school children had come by. Noisy, rude, no different from any others. Hester had terrible cramp that morning and had tried to twitch a shoulder to ease the pain. It had only been a *little* twitch, but it had been enough to topple a plump, freckled lad passing by at the time.

And Hester was *sure* that the boy had noticed her, and so had the maiden who had come to help him up. But boys are nasty things. They throw stones and set their dogs on old women. Maidens aren't much better, she reminded herself. They go snivelling to their dames that the old lady scared them and made the milk turn sour in the churn.

What use was it that two snot-nosed children might have noticed that she was alive and really there? No use whatsoever… Except if *children* could hear, then maybe someone more useful might be able to hear also… someone with the right spells and potions to be able to soften the joints of a poor old woman… Once again she wondered if the naiads had been real, or simply dreams from the years of darkness? They would have been able to help her. Oh what she would have given at that moment for a bowl of rosemary tea with honey and juniper berries! She imagined the warmth beginning to spread through her limbs, and began to cry again.

Just Like Gran 3

Birthday money always burned a hole in Dave's pocket. He pressed his round, pink nose against the window of the computer games shop, leaving a satisfying smear on the glass.

'You'll regret spending all your money on *Deadly Combat*,' Maddy assured him primly. 'You know Mum thinks computer games are a complete waste of money. You'll get square eyes from the screen *and* you'll be bored with it before the week's out *and* it'll be a big disappointment!'

Dave lunged at his sister, taking well-aimed and heartfelt swipes at her with his school bag. With each blow he yelled in no uncertain terms what he thought of her advice.

Maddy just laughed. The few blows that caught her did not hurt. Anyway, she could outrun him easily as he was rather chubby and always got out of breath quickly.

Eventually they both landed panting on a low stone wall to catch their breath. Dave looked downcast. 'I haven't got enough money for what I really want, anyway,' he muttered miserably. 'Lend us £20?'

'No fear! You still owe me £5 from last Christmas!'

'But that was to buy your present with, and you did

want that tape, didn't you? You said it was your best present!'

'Yes, but I didn't expect to have to pay for it myself!' she sniffed derisively. 'Anyway, I've decided to start charging compound interest on my loans. So you now owe me £6, and next week it'll be £7.50, then £10 and so on.'

Dave looked horror-struck. 'But that's not fair!'

Maddy smirked. 'Yes it is; compound interest is how the rich get rich and the poor get poorer! *I* intend to get richer. And if you don't pay up you'll get poorer. *Much* poorer!'

Dave made a face. 'All right, all right! I'll give it to you when we get home. But I'll be really mad if that leaves me short for my other idea.'

'What's that? Some rip-off computer mag? Go on, waste your money—see if I care!' and grabbing her bag she flounced off down the hill towards the small red-brick estate where they lived.

'I want to go back to Wookey Hole to see the witch. I'm sure she's unhappy,' he shouted after her.

Maddy half caught the words as she turned to moan at him for being slow. Her mouth dropped open, and she stopped in the middle of the road, staring like a stranded goldfish.

'Do you really mean that?'

'Of course I do,' he panted, catching up with her.

'So do I.'

The twins stared at each other in amazement.

'Saturday?' ventured Dave.

'I've got swimming until twelve o'clock.'

'Afterwards?'

'It's a deal…' Maddy held out her hand to shake on it.

'But do you think,' Dave looked worried… 'Do you think we're sort of imagining it all… you know, because of Gran dying all alone in the cold and dark the way she did?'

Maddy shivered at the thought. She put her head on one side and thought. 'You mean, we're imagining what we want to imagine because we feel bad about Gran? I know what you mean. But there was nothing we could have done to help her. There was nothing *anyone* could have done. She wouldn't go into a home; she wouldn't come and live with us…'

'That's what she *said*,' Dave began, 'but sometimes I get the nasty feeling that we didn't really want her. I'm certain it's what she felt, so she just said those things to let us off the hook.'

Maddy reddened. 'It would have meant one of us giving up our bedroom and moving into that *cupboard* at the end of the corridor, not that *I* would have minded…' Maddy began, then she trailed off. She had argued more vociferously than anyone against Gran coming to live with them. Maddy's room was freshly decorated just as she really wanted it for the first time ever. The boxroom on the other hand held no such charms. It was small, poky and painted orange.

She swallowed hard and tried again, 'I mean, if only I'd known how really ill she was, I'd have…' She found she had nothing left to say.

Dave just nodded. He felt the same. Anyone would have given up their room if only they'd known… 'But the point is,' he added quietly, 'we can't do any more for our Gran. She's dead, but perhaps we can do something for this old lady?'

Maddy shuddered. 'But she feels so… so

unpleasant… I certainly wouldn't want to give up my room for her, even if she was real, which I doubt.'

Dave shrugged. 'But we could get her a cup of tea or something, couldn't we? I'm sure she'd like that.'

Maddy nodded, but said no more. She had too many conflicting feelings cluttering up her mind. She didn't know why she cared, but she knew she really wanted to do something. The only trouble was the thought of what they were planning felt so—well— *stupid*!

The next Saturday was wet and windy. It was the sort of April day that makes you wonder whether summer will ever actually come.

Despite the danger of being blown off their bikes by the wind, or drowning under a flash-flood, the twins stoically pulled their bikes out from under the rubbish stacked up in the garage and set off towards the caves. The ride from Wells to Wookey Hole was not long, but it was all uphill, and mostly exposed to prevailing gales. Their rucksacks bulged with sandwiches, cartons of drink and extra dry clothing stuffed into plastic bags.

Impressed by the children's sudden interest in local history, Mum had given them extra money to buy post-cards and a guidebook.

The caves were busy that afternoon, and the twins found themselves absorbed into a large tour group. With the perfected skill of teacher-dodgers, the two manoeuvred themselves to the back of the crowd. When they reached the chamber where the stone witch stood, they managed to disappear completely without being noticed, and the tour progressed on.

At last they were alone with the ugly chunk of rock

21

that was called 'the witch'. The twins began to shiver, not just because they were cold and damp from the cycle ride, nor was it because the black, stark profile looked eerie—but because it did remind them of Gran.

Gran had always worn a big, floppy old cap, 'just to keep her brains warm,' she used to say. Then there was the long, hooked nose and a big pointed chin like a Punch puppet. Worst of all, they could imagine the tiny eyes and small mouth lost between the heavy features. It was all so sad.

Behind the figure was a low parapet, designed to keep the public on a safe path. Just below was a steep drop down to an icy green lake at the witch's feet. Maddy leaned over and stretched out a hand to touch the figure's head.

She pulled her hand back quickly. 'Ouch!'

'What's the matter, Mads? Hurt yourself?'

'No, it's just she's so cold, really cold, and lonely. It's horrid. You feel!'

Dave tried, but instead of pulling back, he let his hand rest on the back of the knobbly head. 'You know,' he said, 'I'm sure I felt her move, just a tiny bit.'

Suddenly Maddy snorted in the special way she reserved for silly comments. 'This is ridiculous! Look at us! Look what we're doing! Going all gaga over an old lump of rock. Let's go home; I'm cold.'

But Dave was scrambling down the rocks to the side of the path. He was dangerously close to the edge of the water. Precariously balanced, he clung with one hand to the back of the figure, while with the other hand he rummaged in his rucksack until he found his much loved Liverpool scarf. Laboriously, he began to twist it around the witch's thick, bent neck.

Maddy leaned over the parapet and called down, 'What on earth are you doing? You'll be murdered if you're caught.'

'She's cold, like you said.' Dave gave the scarf another tug. 'I just don't want her to be cold any more. It hurts to think about it.'

Maddy didn't hesitate. 'Take my scarf instead. It's old and doesn't matter. Dad bought you that Liverpool one for Christmas, and he'll be hopping mad if you lose it.'

Dave obediently unwound the precious scarf and reached up for the old, pink, hand-knitted one that Maddy was dangling down to him. Suddenly they heard voices… another tour was coming!

Maddy darted to her left and hid behind a huge sta-lagmite that looked like a frozen waterfall of cream. Her left foot slipped and landed in an ice-cold pool of water. The wetness seeped through the eyelets and into her socks. Freezing drops of water plopped from the rocks above onto her head, and began to crawl down the back of her neck. She dared not move or make a sound. She must not let herself care. She hoped that Dave had found a spot to hide as well.

She hated rows, and trying to explain to a guide what they were doing would be awkward to say the least.

In fact Dave was crouched below the witch. His feet stuck out awkwardly and he could tell he was about to get cramp all down one side. He closed his eyes and thought of his last visit to the dentist in minute detail. Soon all other discomforts faded into insignificance…

The visitors clattered and clambered close to the

guide to hear how this place was once thought to be the entrance to hell. Red lights were flickering and thunderous sound effects roared and echoed. Dave realized with horror that he was curled up right next to one of the speakers, and he stuffed his fingers in his ears until they hurt.

It was then that he saw he had dropped his Liverpool scarf. There it lay, right underneath the very feet of the witch, in full view of everyone. He muttered something unrepeatable under his breath and closed his eyes. He half hoped that if *he* couldn't see it, then perhaps the tourists wouldn't see it either: although he knew that was nonsense.

But the scarf was spotted, and some wag made a joke about the witch being a Liverpool supporter. The guide asked the people to wait, and he slipped quickly and sure-footedly down to where the scarf lay. At that moment he looked up to where Dave was crouched…

The guide opened his mouth to say something, when suddenly an awful cracking sound echoed ominously all around.

One or two of the more nervous people screamed, and others tried to run away in different directions. The guide immediately forgot about Dave. He twisted the scarf around his own neck and in three bounds he was back up on the main walkway.

Panting to catch his breath, he spoke calmly to his group, calling back the wanderers, assuring them there was no danger. He told them that the noise was an echo from a fault much deeper in the caves, then quickly and firmly he steered his little flock on to the next chamber.

What a close shave! The scarf was gone; the guide

had it! Dave would have to go to the shop and say he'd dropped it somewhere during a tour. With any luck he might not have been spotted. Slipping and sliding dangerously, he clambered back up to the walkway and called out to his sister.

For one, long, panic-stricken moment there was silence. Then, 'Dave?'

Maddy uncurled herself and ventured out of her hiding-place, wincing as the bitterly cold water squelched between her toes. 'Dave... the witch moved! I saw it! That was what caused the cracking noise. It wasn't a fault in the caves. Honestly! The poor old thing's got arthritis!'

'Just like Gran,' Dave added softly. 'Let's get out of here, I don't like it.'

Wishes 4 Granted

The twins tried to cheer themselves up by dawdling in the fairground displays and mirror maze housed in the old paper-mill below the caves. Because of their birthday, they had plenty of money for once, and Dave was convinced that he was onto a winning streak with the old-fashioned slot-machines.

Maddy had always wanted a photograph of herself in an old Wild West costume. Her dream was to have been Calamity Jane. The photographer was just putting the finishing touches to the pose when Dave rushed across the hall. He was hot, bothered, and looking rounder and pinker than ever.

With a huge effort at ignoring him, Maddy kept her pose, hand on hip, bottle on the table and a heavy gun touted at all comers. But her fierce glare at Dave, daring him to intrude on her moment of glory, was now preserved for posterity.

As the camera shutter clicked, Maddy stamped her foot hard. 'What on earth's the matter? You are a beast. I bet you've spoiled my picture now!'

She flounced off into the changing cubicle, leaving Dave hopping from foot to foot and flapping his arms like a chicken ready to lay. 'Do hurry, Mads! You are such a slow coach! Boys don't make a fuss about changing; they just fling everything off and then put something else on!'

'And leave it where you flung it?' came Maddy's muffled voice.

'Of course! What else? But please hurry—this is important!'

It was so unlike Dave to say 'please' voluntarily that she did hurry. She folded the cowboy's leather overtrousers and pulled on her baggy purple sweatshirt as fast as possible.

As her round face appeared from behind the curtains she shook out her thick mane of light brown hair. 'Well, what is it? Has the cat had kittens?'

Dave tugged at her arm, 'You'll have to come and see. I can't explain just like that.'

Maddy stuffed her wet socks into her rucksack. 'You'll have to hold on a mo. I must put dry socks on.' When she stood up he was gone. What a pest he was!

There was no sign of him amongst the slot-machines where he had been playing earlier. Laboriously she wound her way through the mirror maze. Still no Dave. Then she found herself in the fairground section. Everywhere was alive with barrel-organ music, coloured lights and excited children.

At last Maddy spotted her brother hunched over a dusty glass display case. Coming up behind him she elbowed him firmly out of the way so she could see what all the fuss was about. Inside the box was an old-fashioned automaton doll dressed as a wizard, complete with a tall, pointed black hat, a long white beard and an aged black cloak that was embroidered with rusty sequins and strange symbols sewn in silver thread. In the wizard's hand was a tarnished silver wand, and in front of the case was a neat white card that read:

Wishes Granted. 1d.

'What's 1d?' Maddy asked, bemused.

'One old penny, dope. Look, I've got just one left!' and he held up a large, dark brown coin that was the currency of the arcade. 'I won loads earlier, then I lost them all. I saved this last one because I thought it might be useful!'

'What are you babbling on about?' Maddy sniffed disdainfully, as Dave pushed his last coin into the slot. Then she held her breath as Dave spoke clearly into the mouthpiece…

'Please, may the witch come alive again!'

A jingly tune played and the automaton whirred and jerked into life. With the help of wires and little wooden rods working him from behind a threadbare screen, the old wizard doffed his pointed hat and pulled out a card which he then dropped into a little pot in front of him. Then, with a slight click, the neat ivory card landed in a polished brass tray below the glass case.

Dave picked it up with sweaty hands and turned it over. He stared at it for long seconds before Maddy pushed her face over his shoulder. 'Well, what does it say?' she demanded.

Dave pushed the card under Maddy's snub nose. On it, in old-fashioned copperplate were the words:

Your wish will come true… but you won't like it!

She took the card and looked at it. She turned it over and then shrugged as she handed it back. 'Well, what does that mean?'

28

'I don't know, but I don't like it!' Dave shivered. 'It feels even worse than the caves. I wish I'd got another penny to unwish it.'

Maddy just laughed. 'Don't be daft. You can't "unwish" wishes; they just don't work like that.'

'How do you know?'

'Well, in stories they don't.'

'Do you believe in wishes then?' Dave was looking very worried.

'Well, they're not very scientific, are they?' Maddy looked at the card again, and went to toss it in a nearby bin.

'Don't do that!' Dave looked quite pale.

'Why, what's the matter? It's only a bit of printed card from a machine—it won't *mean* anything. It's not real, is it?'

But Dave wasn't listening. He had gone quite white. He was staring at the grimly approaching figure of a long-haired cave guide, draped in a Liverpool supporter's scarf.

'Oops!' Dave whispered. 'I think we're in for trouble.'

The Offering

The lanky young guide simply handed Dave the scarf.
'If you drop anything again, just get one of us to fetch
it. Don't go clambering around again, or you'll be
banned from the caves. That water is deadly cold.
Literally. If you'd slipped in, it could easily have been
the end of you.'

The young man looked kind, and genuinely worried
for Dave. 'I mean it,' he said. 'The legends about
people going into the caves and not coming out again
because the witch got them are based on fact. One
foot in the wrong place in a cave and you've had it.'

Dave opened his mouth to make an excuse, but
found himself blurting out, 'But it's not like that, she's
real! She's alive!'

Maddy kicked her brother firmly in the ankle, but he
did not retaliate. In fact he ignored her completely and
blurted out the whole story. She slunk off to sit behind
a display where she could hear everything, and not be
too embarrassed by having such a dork-brain for a
brother.

The guide sat silently on the edge of a merry-go-
round and looked up at Dave. The boy was short and
plump with a pleasant face and a very straight gaze. He
was not goofing around. At last the guide sighed.

'Listen, there is no witch. The tales were made up to scare silly kids away from the caves because they're dangerous. There were probably lots of old ladies who lived up there at one time or another, some dotty, others not. The "Witch of Wookey Hole" is a stumpy stalagmite—nothing more, nothing less. I hate to say this to someone I don't know, but you're talking non-sense, and the sooner you go out in the fresh air, the better for you, the better for everyone.'

Then he smiled kindly and handed Dave some coins. 'Why don't you and your friend who's hiding over there go and have an ice-cream on me?'

Maddy could see from her vantage point that Dave was on the verge of tears. He might be her obnoxious twin brother, but he was genuine. Her conscience pricked her. She couldn't let him take this all by him-self. The guide was very kind, but he had to know that Dave was telling the truth.

Her heart was pounding hard as she stepped out. 'I'm his sister, not his friend, and everything he says is true.' She looked the man levelly in the eye, and to her horror felt herself going very, very red.

The guide looked at the two very sincere faces in front of him and sighed as he sat down again. For a few moments he said nothing, but sat with his head in his hands. At last he sighed and looked up.

'OK kids, listen; this is what I will do for you. I'm off duty now, but be here at twelve o'clock tomorrow. Are you free?'

The twins nodded.

'Fine. I'll take you round as my guests—no need to pay this time. Just tell whoever's on the till that you're friends of Tim, and they'll let you through. Then, as we go, I'll let you look carefully and you'll see there is no such thing as the Witch of Wookey Hole. Then you can drop this silly notion. Is that a deal?'

Dave hung his head. He wasn't sure he could promise to drop something that was true. But he *could* promise to come and look properly. 'Deal' he said at last, and held out his hand to shake on it. Maddy did the same, giving as grateful a smile as she could manage, but she did not feel very happy at all.

Mum was astounded. 'You're going up the caves *again*?'

'Yeah, there was this guide who saw we were really interested, and he offered to take us round for free this time!' Dave was standing at the door, hopping from foot to foot, wishing that Mum would stop asking questions and let them go. It was already 11.40 a.m.; they had to be there at the main gate by twelve o'clock.

'It's very nice of him, but don't get in the way, will you dear?' Mum was very into educational trips and going round places, but she was also convinced that something was up— three visits to the same place in less than a week was downright suspicious.

'No, Mum. Of course we won't be in the way.' Dave replied absently. 'Maddy, hurry *UP*!'

Maddy started to run downstairs. Then she disappeared again. 'Just a minute, I've forgotten something vital.' And she reappeared clasping a string of pink coral around her neck. 'OK, I'm ready now.'

'Fancy bothering to put on a *necklace* for going to the caves!' Dave muttered. 'It's not a birthday party you know!'

Maddy just shrugged as she yanked her bike out from under Dave's. 'I can wear what I like.' She was too embarrassed to admit what she was planning to do. Dave would think she was nuts.

The twins missed the twelve o'clock tour. They met up with their guide coming up the steep path to the main entrance at 12.30 p.m. 'Sorry, Mum kept asking us questions and we couldn't get out.'

'Very sensible of her,' Tim smiled. '"Where are you going?" and "Who are you going with?" I bet. Never mind, you're here now. You're lucky—there's only six others, so you can take your time and poke around a bit. Now, try to behave will you? I don't want to get into trouble because of you. I need this job.'

They both promised and followed Tim quite meekly. As they passed the witch-stone, neither of them said anything, but Maddy did reach out and touch the figure's head, which was quite cold and hard. Just as a good stalagmite should be. Yet far from being convinced that the witch was not real, she only felt sad because the old woman must be incredibly cold and lonely. On an impulse, Dave left a few toffees on a knob of stone next to the unmoving figure. They were carefully chosen because they were slightly less mucky than the others in the gloomy depths of his trouser pocket. It took a very dexterous manoeuvre to slip the sweets down onto the stone without Tim noticing, but Dave chose his moment well, when plenty of thunder and lightning were being flashed around the chamber as Tim told his tales.

The guide did not give any sign that he noticed anything, and the twins followed him on their best behaviour, listening with rapt attention as he went through his now-familiar routine and stories, switching the lights and sounds to produce stunning effects as they walked. But in the whirlpool chamber, just as he was relating how the ancient Celts seemed to have used the chamber to make offerings to their god, the River, Maddy threw something into the waters. At least, that was what Dave suspected happened.

Tim darted threatening glances at the children, but Dave picked up a small pebble and tossed it into the water. It made a satisfying 'plop' sound, but not quite the same as whatever Maddy had thrown in.

Tim glowered at the twins again. Dave shrugged and grinned. 'Just seeing if it's easy to skim pebbles here. The water looks so smooth it looks as if you ought to be able to bounce a good one four or five times.'

Tim said nothing, but made an 'I'm still watching you' sort of face and continued describing how, in exceptionally wet weather, the water sometimes rose and flooded the chamber in a tremendous whirlpool, which over the years had carved the strange shallow dome out of the rock above.

Maddy looked up. The ceiling looked so low that she felt she ought to be able to touch it. The chamber had a strange feeling of being almost warm and inti- mate, a place that was full and alive, as well as terrifying for its terrible power. Once caught in there with the water rising to the roof in less than twenty minutes, who could tell what would happen? Perhaps this was why in ages past people had come here to worship their gods.

Maddy stood quite still trying to imagine how things had been, while the others moved on.

Tim turned back and saw her standing alone at the bottom of the steps. 'Come on Maddy, time to go.'

She shook herself awake, but as she turned to climb the metal staircase out of the chamber, a soft, gentle voice chanted, 'You must want your wish to come true very much to give me such a pretty gift. What is it you want?'

Maddy turned, and gripped the cold iron bannister very tightly with her right hand until her knuckles hurt. Her heart was pounding. She felt hot and clammy, and very frightened. Who was speaking? She hadn't really expected anything to happen. She just thought that maybe, if she gave something she really treasured, like people did in ancient times, then maybe, just maybe, the witch might come to life again. Although she knew it made no sense at all.

Her coral necklace was the most 'watery' gift she could think of to give to the river, and now this voice had spoken. Such a soft, gentle voice, the sound of a stream in a warm valley on a summer's day. It was a good voice, it was the sound of laughing, life-giving water. Not a raging river god in full torrential rage. She plucked up all her courage as she turned to answer.

'I wish the witch could become warm again.'

Because 6 of Gran

Tim gave no sign that he had seen or heard anything at the whirlpool chamber, other than Dave throwing stones into the water. At the end of the tour, the twins thanked him politely and handed him some chocolate they had bought as a thank-you present. Then they ran down to the old paper-mill and towards the fairground exhibits as quickly as possible.

They did not want to be asked any awkward questions about the witch. They had no answers.

'Did you hear that voice in the whirlpool chamber?' Maddy whispered at last as they entered the glittering hall of carousels and magnificent barrel-organs.

'I heard something, but I wasn't sure whether it was a stream laughing or a voice.'

'I know what you mean, it sounded like... like one of those golden naiads would sound like,' Maddy said, pointing to a gracefully carved lady, holding up one of the edges of a fairground canopy. Her father, Neptune, ruler of all waters, was shaped as the central pillar.

'More like it was our imagination, Mads,' Dave muttered. 'There's nothing there. Tim is right. We've got to grow up. Calcium carbonate is calcium carbonate, and lonely old ladies live in flats, not caves.'

'But it needn't be!' Maddy answered. 'I mean, who's

to say it's not possible she's real? Miracles *ought* to be able to happen, after all. And as for witches, I think if she was really evil, we wouldn't feel sorry for her. We wouldn't want to go back and make her warm. We'd want to run away as fast as we could. If there ever was an old lady there, I don't think she was an evil witch. I think she was lonely and frightened and someone whom no one cared about. She may have been unpleasant and cross, but not bad.'

Maddy trailed off her speech. Dave wasn't listening. He was staring at the glass case that held the wizard's automaton, the one that had 'wishes granted' written neatly on a card. The doll's cracked and battered face was leering at the children as it rocked backwards and forwards and dropped another card into the little brass tray below.

Happy now?

it asked in the same neat copperplate as before. But the writing was smudged. The ink was wet. This was no pre-printed card.

'Maddy,' he whispered, as he picked the card up between his finger and thumb, 'I didn't put any money in this thing; it wrote the card all by itself…'

His sister turned very slightly so she could watch the automaton from the corner of her eye. She glanced at Dave and swallowed hard. 'It's not the witch that makes me feel spooky. It's this thing!'

'Me too!' Dave replied, shivering. He was quite white as he looked at the message again. Then, screwing up his face in a very determined way, he began to tear the card into minute pieces. He tossed them into the nearest bin. But as he did so, someone, somewhere opened a door and the shredded card rose in the draught and the pieces flew back into his face.

Maddy caught her breath as Dave flapped the shreds away from his eyes. 'Let's go home,' she said.

'I'm going to sell my *Gameboy*.' Dave announced suddenly after tea.

Maddy was doing her homework and she was not really listening. 'What?'

'I'm going to sell it. I've got to get back to the caves, and I've run out of money. I can't see a way round it. Snotty Cotham offered me a tenner for it last week.'

'Mum'll be mad—you moaned and moaned for that thing!'

'That was two years ago. But I've got to do it, Mads.'

Maddy put down her pen and looked at her brother. 'But *why*?'

'I just told you. Because I've got to go back to the caves again. For Gran's sake.'

'What has she got to do with it?' Maddy scratched her head with the end of her pen and got ink on her fingers. She started to scrub at the blotches with a much-used tissue.

Dave reddened. 'I thought you'd understand.' Then he turned back to his geography worksheets.

'Well I might if you explained.'

Dave wasn't in a mood for explaining. Once he'd been embarrassed, he generally clammed up and that was that.

Maddy could feel his mood. He was hurt. She'd said something wrong, and she wasn't sure what. But it was to do with the caves, and Gran, so it was important to her. It was worth trying to win him round with a bit of an apology, so she rummaged in her bag for her last piece of gum.

She tossed it over to him. 'Here. Look, I'm sorry I wasn't really listening. I've been threatened with death if I get this maths wrong again. Now, I've put my pen down, and I'm all ears. Please tell me again, why are you selling your *Gameboy*?'

Dave unwrapped the gum very, very slowly. He was quite red around the ears. Would Maddy laugh at him? He had to tell her. He'd need her help, after all.

'It's Gran. I feel bad about the way she died all alone, and I'm sure the witch is alive. I want to help her come alive and look after her.' Then he was silent for a second. At last he looked up, his wide eyes appealing not to be mocked. 'I let Gran down, and I knew what she was feeling, all lonely and stuff. But I didn't *do* anything. I could have done something. I know she insisted that she was all right, but I knew how scared she was inside. I should have spoken up and I didn't.

'Now I'm sure I've found someone else who feels almost the same as Gran, and it's not too late to help. It's a way of sort of making it up to Gran I suppose.'

Then he shoved the gum in his mouth and chewed furiously, burying his head in his work. He could feel his face and ears going red, and he wished he'd never spoken, but it was said. Now Maddy would have a good laugh at him, as she usually did.

There was a long silence as Maddy stared at the ceiling. 'What can we *do* though?' she said at last.

'Well, I'm going to leave her some sandwiches and a flask of hot tea, for a start!' Dave spoke very quickly, as if he was scared he wasn't going to get all his words out before he changed his mind.

'And some biscuits for the dog,' Maddy added, getting excited.

'What's Mum going to say?'

Maddy sat back on her heels and chewed the end of her pencil. 'I suppose we needn't say anything—yet?'

'Bit difficult not to. She'll want to know where we're going and so on.'

'We could do the caves as our local history project, then Mum would let us go there as much as we like. It'd give us the chance to rummage in the museum and see what we can come up with there as well!'

Dave beamed. 'Deal!' he said. 'I was stuck for what to do for the project. That's a brill idea. This way we can tell the truth and Mum and Dad might even be pleased!'

'But we're not going to say anything about the witch…?'

Dave put his head on one side, almost as if he was listening. 'No, not yet. If she actually comes alive, we'll have to, but not yet…'

Maddy looked serious. 'I feel the same. I don't want to be thought of as barmy—not until there's something to show for it!'

By discreetly asking at the gift shop, the twins learned that Tim's day off was a Wednesday. They did not want to bump into him, so they cycled up to the caves after school, certain that he would not be there. They just made it in time for the last tour of the day.

As they came to the chamber where the witch sat, the children waited for the thunder and lightning show, when they knew the guide would flash lights and make a terrible noise as he told them how people used to believe this place was the entrance to hell.

That was their cue.

Swiftly, Maddy laid the biscuits in front of the 'dog' stalagmite, and Dave pushed a packet of cheese sandwiches and a flask of tea in front of the 'witch' stone. Then they were back in their places, looking as if butter wouldn't melt in their mouths by the time the sound-and-light show had finished.

It was only a matter of about twenty seconds, but they did it.

However, as the noise and light finished, a thin, irritable voice spoke… 'And about time too!'

The guide looked around, wondering who had spoken, but the children were busily (and loudly) discussing why the surrounding rocks were streaked different colours in such interesting ways.

The guide happily took up the theme and forgot the voice.

Dave and Maddy were so scared they could not get out of the caves fast enough. They slipped in all the puddles and muddy patches, and tripped over every rough bit of floor. The walkways over the deep water in caverns 23 and 24 had never seemed so terrifying. They had their hearts in their mouths every step of the way, and by the time they were out in the air again, they were sweating with fear.

'I am never, never, going in there again!' Maddy muttered as she drew breath, feeling the air of the fine spring evening filling her lungs.

'Nor am I!' Dave promised.

The following Sunday they happened to meet Tim in town. He looked quite worried and, for once, seemed willing to talk about the witch.

'We might have to close the caves,' he confided, 'although it's all hush-hush at the moment.'

Dave and Maddy exchanged glances. They both had a feeling they could guess what was coming next. Maddy swallowed hard. 'Why's that Tim? It'd be awful…' she was about to say 'for the witch,' but Dave chipped in. 'Awful for everyone. It's a terrific place to go.'

Tim shrugged. 'Well, there have been so many accidents there lately. We've had experts down from London, but they can't make head or tail of it. There are faults in the rocks, obviously—that's the nature of caves—but the ground keeps shaking and grinding in the most frightening way. People are often knocked off their feet. Then there's an almost perpetual sound of crying. We think there must be a new pothole widening at the surface and the prevailing wind is whistling in. We can't think where else it's coming from.'

'Where is the sound loudest?' Dave ventured, almost not daring to hear the answer.

'Mostly it's in the chamber where the "witch" stalagmite is, but at times it can be heard almost everywhere. We're all baffled. Some people have been hurt quite badly and are threatening legal action. It's dreadful.'

Dave bit his lip and hung his head. He felt bad. They had wished the witch to come alive, then they had left her all alone without being there for her when she woke up. That was a terrible thing to do to anyone. They had failed in their plan of helping the witch for their Gran's sake.

When Dave looked up, he was shocked to see that Maddy was grinning. She gave him a sharp nudge. 'I'd like to see this; we're doing a report on the caves for history!'

'But no mention of the cave closing?' Tim asked warily.

'None whatsoever, I promise. You can see what I write before it goes in if you like. I won't even mention the tremors. I'll just write about the eerie crying sound, "Has the witch come to life?" and all that stuff.'

She looked up at Tim and grinned in such a winning way that he found it hard to say anything cross. But he felt it. 'I thought you two had grown out of all that nonsense,' he frowned.

'Oh come on Tim, it's just a bit of fun…?'

Tim met them at the caves that afternoon. He took the twins in as his guests, although he warned he couldn't keep doing it for them.

When Dave and Maddy arrived they were drenched. It was a cold, wet day. It had been tempting to stay at home and watch the telly. Although Maddy and Dave turned up, everyone else in the world it seemed, preferred the telly option. The twins were alone at the guide's gatehouse.

Tim came up the steep path and greeted the children with a cheery wave. 'I think you two are going to be disappointed; there've been no mysterious crying sounds at all today. But then the wind is in a different direction from usual.'

'Yeah,' Maddy grinned as she wrung the water out of her hair, 'It's blowing from the bottom of the Bristol Channel, and it's bringing most of the water up with it!'

Tim unlocked the gate and stepped inside, starting his tour in the usual way, shining the little green 'witch-light' torch all around. Then he stopped. 'I feel daft saying all this just for you two. You know it all anyway.

'How about we just walk around and listen—and see what happens?' Maddy asked hopefully, catching sight of Dave out of the corner of her eye. He looked decidedly ill.

'That's what I was going to suggest,' Tim replied, putting his 'witch-torch' into the copious pocket of his overalls. Then he strode ahead, ducking the over-hanging rocks, leaving the twins behind in the half-light.

Maddy hung back and grabbed Dave by the arm. 'What's the matter? You look dreadful!' she whispered.

Dave swallowed and clutched his throat. 'Think I'm going to be sick,' he moaned.

'Let's get you out in the fresh air!' Maddy started to tug her brother back towards the entrance, 'I'll tell Tim we're going…'

'No! Don't!' Dave insisted, 'it's… it's… oh, you'll see!' And he started to run to catch the guide up, his short legs slipping and struggling on the wet steps.

At the bottom Tim was staring out across the parapet, his mouth open in disbelief.

'I knew it,' Dave muttered, struggling not to heave, 'I just *knew* something had happened!'

'What's happened?' Maddy demanded, breathlessly, bumping into Dave as she jumped down the last couple of steps into the witch's 'skullery'.

Dave turned, white as a sheet. 'It's the witch, Mads—look!'

The 7 Witch

In place of the witch-stone was a very miserable, smelly, scrawny old lady. Standing in the middle of the path behind the parapet, she looked a pathetic sight. Her arms were as thin as matchsticks, and her huge head was topped with a great mob cap. Her beaky nose was bent down towards her chin and tiny, black, piercing eyes darted and glanced, taking in everything, missing nothing. The old lady was dressed in a threadbare grey smock that reached down to the ground, but around her neck she had Maddy's pink scarf tied very firmly. She looked funny, but no one dared laugh.

As Tim and the twins approached, a very lanky, snarling black dog got up from where it was crouching to the left of the stone staircase and took a few steps towards them. It lowered its bony head and barked twice, threateningly.

The old woman turned round and snapped at the dog. 'Bledig, shut it! I told you before not to behave like that when there be cump'ny.' And she raised her hand as if she was about to wallop him.

The dog whimpered and crawled back into the shadows, obviously terrified.

The strange figure then turned her attention to the visitors. 'An' where 'ave you bin? I be hungry, an' I bain't had vittals since that bit o' bread and cheese yestere'en. 'Snot goodenuff, it bain't!'

The children stepped back a pace, and Tim spread his hands protectively in front of them. 'Don't panic, kids; we get all sorts of weirdos in here. I'll get the police to move her. I don't think she's dangerous, but the dog might be…' and with that he gripped the children firmly by their shoulders and tried to turn them around.

But they wouldn't budge. Dave wriggled free from Tim's grasp. 'But don't you *see*, Tim—it's *her*. The witch I mean…'

The old woman glared at the boy. 'Oi! Who's bin tellin' fibs on me then? Who sez I'm a witch? Tell me an' I'll turn 'em into a frog. I bain't 'avin' that sorta gossip! Tin't true an' tin't fair nivver!' And with that she stuck her pointed chin defiantly in the air and stared at them all with angry eyes.

The trio were so taken aback by the tirade that they all stood stock-still with their mouths hanging open. At last Dave tried again… 'Excuse me, are you the… the er *lady* that normally sits here on this rock?' he gestured lamely towards the knobbly outcrop on the lake side of the parapet, where, until so recently, there had always been a witch-stone.

The old lady pulled herself up to her full height (which wasn't very much) and glared at them. 'Wot if I be?' she snapped.

Dave took another step forward and held out a hand. 'We're very pleased to meet you, Miss…'

He broke off as the crouching dog gave a warning snarl. Terrified, Dave jumped back. The old lady screeched, *'BLEDIG!'* with such vehemence that the

46

great animal cowered again and lay quite flat on the cold, wet rock floor.

Then, very stiffly, the old lady leaned forward and held out a claw-like hand and scowled. But she had no intention of shaking hands. 'So where be me supper then?' she demanded.

Maddy was infuriated. 'Don't you ever say "please" or "thank you"?'

The old woman's head snapped round to glare at the girl. 'Wot for?'

Maddy had no answer to this. The old lady's rudeness threw her completely. So she just shrugged and said, 'Well, what sort of supper do you usually like?'

The old woman stepped forward again and pinched Maddy's arm rather painfully. 'Nice plump maiden'd do a treat!' and she opened her huge, gaping mouth and laughed, breathing the stink of rotten teeth and foul breath all over Maddy.

Tim had had enough of the old woman. He put his arms protectively around the children and very calmly said, 'Now, Miss...?'

'Me name's Hester Wookey as if yer didn't know!' she snapped.

'Miss Wookey, if you are the... young lady who usually sits here, we'll be glad to fetch you some supper. Would chicken sandwiches do?'

'Wot's a "sandy witch"?' The old crone peered up at Tim and breathed her fetid odour over him too. 'We only eats chiddern, you know; we don't eat each uvver! I bain't eatin' no sandy witch, nor no rock nor water witch nivver!'

Tim sighed. This was going to be very hard work. 'A sandwich is something nice to eat between two thin bits of bread. How do you fancy chicken and bread for example?'

'Yea, I likes a bitta chicken. And while yer at it, I wants more of this stuff,' and she leaned over the parapet and pulled out the Thermos that Dave had filled with tea and left for her on the last visit.

'Certainly, Miss Wookey,' Tim said, taking the flask which was now covered with gritty, sticky toffee smears. 'But I beg you, don't move from here. Stay exactly where you usually sit, or we might not be able to get back in. If the people that own this place think you've gone, they'll say it's dangerous and close it, and we won't be able to get back in at all. Then you'll be really hungry.'

Hester Wookey poked Tim hard in the stomach with a twiggy forefinger. 'Wot's in it for me?'

Maddy shoved a pack of boiled sweets under Miss Wookey's face. 'Here, suck these while you're waiting—they're really nice.'

Hester grabbed the packet in her claw and shovelled three sweets in at once, but made a face and spat them straight out again. 'UGH! You tryin' to poison me or summat?'

Maddy looked at the spat-out sweets with regret. They had been expensive, and she had been looking forward to them. Then she had a moment's inspiration. She bent over and picked one of the slimy balls up, and gingerly undid the cellophane. 'I think you're supposed to take the wrappers off first, Miss Wookey,' she suggested kindly. 'Otherwise it's...' she struggled to find an analogy that Hester would understand, something from her own century. 'Otherwise it's like trying to eat an egg with its shell still on,' she suggested.

'How else do you eat eggs, then?' Hester snapped as she took the sweet and popped it into her mouth. But, despite her bad temper, a look of glowing pleasure did spread across her face as the sweet taste melted around her shrivelled old gums.

Tim looked at his watch. 'Listen, we've got to move. The place is supposed to be cleared by now. The chief guide will be walking round inspecting everything and making sure there's no idiots trying to camp out here for the night. Miss Wookey, I strongly advise that if you want us to be able to come back, and if you want to be sure not to be thrown out yourself, you'll return to your seat and keep immobile. And try and keep the dog under control as well. We'll be back first thing in the morning. The doors will be locked in a few minutes, so we can't get back in tonight, even if we wanted to.'

'Eeh? Wot's 'e saying?' Hester looked quizzically from one child to the other.

Maddy leaned over and kindly unwrapped another sweet for the old lady. 'He says, if you know what's good for you, you'll stay quite still and shut up.'

The old woman climbed back down to her little ledge and glowered at her visitors resentfully. 'You're tryin' to trick me. I can smell it you know. You can't fool ol' Hester Wookey. I'll rack you all with agues and cramps so you never sleep a wink for the rest of your lives if you don't cum back. I warned you now!'

And with that she settled back to her old pose, the one she had held for so many centuries, and for all the world, if it hadn't been for Maddy's pink scarf around her neck, it looked as if she had never moved.

Maddy glanced nervously over her shoulder at the

dog who had crouched sullenly in his corner. Bledig watched the visitors' every move with a malicious pair of yellow eyes. Maddy shivered. 'Time to go home, I think.'

Hester's New Outfit

Dad wasn't pleased with the idea, but Maddy wasn't about to give up.

'Oh go on Dad. There's bags of the stuff, all just sitting in the attic getting eaten by mice and moths while someone thinks what to do with it all. Now at last here's a good use.'

Dad shook his head. 'It's not just rubbish… It's my Mum's clothes. It's sort of still all rather close to me. Can't your friend get some stuff from a charity shop for his gran?'

'He's got no money,' Dave answered ruefully—and honestly, pushing his hand into his pocket to rattle around for his very last few coins. If Tim ever stopped sneaking them into the caves, they'd be sunk. They couldn't afford another entrance fee this side of Christmas. Then who would look after Miss Wookey?

Mum came into the sitting-room. 'What's the matter? Who's got no money? Surely not you, Dave; you had loads for your birthday.'

Dave reddened. 'Well, not exactly. This old lady I know—we know, I mean… She's sort of a friend of ours. Well, she lives in this really damp, cold place, and she's literally got no money…'

Maddy chimed in, 'And she needs some new clothes—or better ones, at least. Hers are really old…'

'Really, *really* old,' Dave added, with feeling.

'And we wondered if we could have some of Gran's old bits in the attic?'

'But Dad says no,' Dave finished off. 'He says he doesn't like some other lady wearing his mum's clothes.'

'Well, I can understand that,' Mum smiled. 'But there was a load of stuff that Gran herself had bundled up for the charity shop before she died. Perhaps Dad would let your old lady have some of those.'

Dad nodded, but still looked sad. 'I don't see why not,' he conceded at last. 'Even she had thrown them out. They can't have been important to her. And there is a *lot* of stuff in the attic. You're quite right. I can't keep it all.'

Early the next morning, Tim sneaked the children past the chief guide. All three were carrying well-stuffed plastic bags. Tim's contained chicken sandwiches, a flask of sweet tea and a chocolate cake.

Dave's bag rattled with two tins of dog food, a tin opener and a packet of dog biscuits.

Maddy's was the biggest, bulgiest bag. She and Dave had sorted through Gran's 'throw outs' in the attic. Gran had been quite a big woman, and Hester Wookey was tiny, like a human spider, all skinny legs and arms, so finding something she could wear was quite difficult. At last they chose a pretty print dress which could be made tighter with a belt, a green woolly cardigan and purple, flowery slippers.

Maddy protested that no-one would be seen dead in

slippers like those, but Dave insisted that they took them.

They had got up very early to go to the caves to meet Tim so they could deliver their bags and still be at school on time. But what should have been a quick trip just to drop the things off soon turned into a marathon task—and they were very late for school indeed.

When they arrived at Hester's cavern, it was the smell that hit them first. It was the sickly sweet stink of fresh blood mixed with the stench of singed feathers. As they came down the steps, the huge black dog rose up and slunk towards them, head down, ears back, and yellow eyes rolling. His mouth pulled back in a snarl with saliva dripping from his gums.

Hester was sitting on her stone perch, pulling at a raw chicken with her few remaining teeth. She was surrounded by feathers and discarded, half-chewed bones. She vaguely looked up as the visitors stopped nervously on the steps. '*BLEDIG!*' she screeched. 'I told you before, shuttit!' Then she tossed a bit of raw chicken carcass at him. He took it to the back of the chamber and crunched it noisily between his teeth.

'Wot took yer so long?' Hester muttered, snorting and wiping the snot across the back of her hand.

Maddy was horrified. 'Miss Wookey, how *could* you do anything so revolting?'

'Wot? Eat? I woz hungry, weren't I? If you lot dun show, wot yer expect a body to do? I popped out and got me own dinner.'

Tim was astounded. 'But *how* did you get out? The doors were all firmly bolted at 5 p.m. yesterday, and I've only just unlocked them!'

Dave stared wide-eyed and awestruck. 'Cor, Miss, did you get out by *magic*?'

'Shows you lot don't know nuffin, don't it? There's lots o' ways outta here, ways only *I* knows. So there! If you lot weren't gonna look after me properly, I gotta look arfter meself. I went and helped meself, didn't I? There's a nice chicken run not far from here, full of nice, fat, juicy little hens.' And she went back to her horrible gnawing and crunching.

Maddy felt sick at such a revolting sight so early in the morning. 'You could at least have *cooked* it!'

'Wot on? I tried, but your fires bain't no good!' And she pointed to a spotlight smeared with bits of chicken flesh. The feathers still stuck to the pieces were singeing, and accounted for quite a lot of the nause-ating smell.

Tim decided it was time to stop this nonsense. He took the raw chicken pieces out of her hands and threw them to Bledig. Then he gave his handkerchief to Maddy and asked her to dip it in a rock pool so Hester could wipe herself down a bit. He was very good with the old lady, talking firmly but gently all the while, assuring her that they would look after her and feed her properly, but she would have to be a good girl and do as she was told for just a few more days, while they sorted out how they were going to do it.

Then he tried to hand her the sandwiches and show her how to peel the cling film off. But she snatched them away from him and tore at the packet with her grimy black fingernails. But when she sunk her few remaining teeth into the nice, soft bread, instead of getting any thanks he was screeched at for not having put mustard on the chicken. Then she shoved the rest

54

of the first sandwich into her mouth, all in one go, and chewed gleefully, shoving stray bits back into her cavernous maw with her very dirty fingers.

The sight made everyone's stomach churn. It was almost as bad as watching her eat the chicken raw. Tim looked at his watch. 'We must go now,' he said. 'There's a party of schoolchildren coming round in a minute.'

'And we're horribly late for school ourselves!' Maddy moaned.

'At least we'll miss maths,' Dave grinned as he opened a tin of dog food and gingerly scraped it out as near to Bledig as he dared go. The hound twitched his nose and growled. Dave stepped back swiftly. While the animal was busy with the food, Tim cleared up the remaining chicken bones and feathers.

Maddy showed Hester the clothes and slippers. She was trying to explain to the old lady that she had to stay just as she was, absolutely still and wearing her old things while people were coming round, but she could put on the pretty clothes when the caves were closed. However, all she got in response was 'a fat lot of good it is givin' me stuff I can't wear, then, innit?' Then she grinned. 'So what'll youz do if I wants to go for a walk in my pretties and show off a bit?' The old lady narrowed her eyes and put her head on one side. 'Wot's in it for me? Why should I stay all still-like just to keep you lot out of trouble?'

But the sounds of excited children made Tim panic. 'Hurry you two. Look, Miss Wookey, you can't run about just as you like. People have paid good money to see you; you can't let them down!'

'And why can't I? As it 'appens I feels like dancing!' She sprang onto the little parapet behind her with amazing

55

agility and started to do a little jig. 'All me aches and pains 'ave gorn since I bin movin' around. I feels like a young girl again. Dancin' is the best cure for aching joints I's ever knowed. If I sits all still—like agin, I might stiffen up!' Tim looked around for some sort of inspiration.

Suddenly Dave had an idea, 'If you sit still all day, we'll bring you more chicken sandwiches, *with* mustard... *and* a red hat!'

Hester stopped, one leg in mid-air, precariously balanced on a narrow bit of the wall above the ice-cold lake. Her face brightened. 'You mean it? A real red hat?'

Dave nodded. 'Yes, a real red hat!'

The sound of the school party was getting closer every second. They had to get Hester to be good and sit still... *now*! But she wasn't going to be put off that easily. She scowled and put her smelly face very close to Dave's.

'*How* red?' she asked, suspiciously.

'Oh ever so, ever so red,' Maddy promised. 'Only please do sit still, please, *dear* Miss Wookey.'

Hester scowled and sat down, cross but obedient, on her little shelf and settled into place with a lot of moaning and groaning. Tim grabbed the twins' hands and skidded round the next corner as fast as they all could run. As they fled, Maddy caught sight of Hester swinging her skinny legs so she could admire her brand new purple slippers. 'Oh no!' she gasped. 'Every one will *see*!'

Tim shook his head. 'Nothing we can do, Maddy, except hope no one will notice.' He did not sound very convinced. Then he hurried them towards the whirlpool cavern as a shrill voice echoed after them, 'Bledig! Shuttit. I told you before...'

Hester Does a Jig

The red hat was a wild success. Dave had spotted it in Gran's 'throw out bag'—a brilliant scarlet bowler with the brim turned up at one side, and a huge cockade of crimson flowers on the lower side. The effect was dreadful. It was indeed 'ever so red'.

The twins had had to squash the hat flat and post it to Tim with a note saying that they couldn't come for a few days. They had been given a double detention for being so late to school without an excuse (helping an old lady who wasn't feeling very well did not wash with the assistant head as they had no note from Mum to prove it. The first detention was for being late, the second was for telling lies about *why* they were late.) *Then* they had both been grounded for a week by Mum and Dad because of the double detention.

'It's so *unfair!*' yelled Maddy as she slammed her bedroom door and prepared to sulk for the whole seven days.

Dave said very little, but he went around the house being as quiet as a mouse, being as helpful as possible, hoping to be 'let off' for being good. But it was unlikely to work; when Mum and Dad set their minds to a 'grounding', there was no way round it.

To Dave and Maddy it was terribly unjust, but how

could they argue their case? No one would believe them.

When Tim got the hat and the note in the post, he was relieved at first. He was beginning to find it a nuisance to sneak the children into the caves all the time. There was no way *he* could afford to pay their entrance money every day. Secretly he had half hoped that if Maddy and Dave went away, Miss Wookey might disappear as well.

But she did not. In fact she got worse, and very soon Tim was deeply regretting not having the twins around. They were very good with the troublesome old lady who now not only demanded food and plenty of it, but to make matters worse she refused to take the hat off.

Tim managed to get himself on all the early shifts, so he could whip the scarlet and crimson creation away from Miss Wookey before anyone else spotted the supposed stalagmite wearing it. Tim then had to threaten not to give it back unless she stayed as still as stone. This made the poor old lady very weepy and unhappy and Tim hated doing it.

He almost wished that Dave had never given the old lady the wretched hat. He certainly *really* wished Dave and Maddy had never brought the witch to life. But he often thought as he looked at the bent, lonely shape of Hester Wookey as she stayed still for the visitors, that bringing a witch to life must need something stronger than a little wooden wizard's magic. Perhaps Miss Wookey would have come to life anyway? Perhaps something stronger was at work. There were always strange feelings and sounds in the Hole; who knew what ancient things lurked down there?

The following Sunday the twins were set free at last. They cadged the entrance fee for the caves from Dad on the grounds that they had to go as they were studying Wookey Hole for their school project. Truth to tell, Mum was glad to get rid of them for a few hours. Grounding the children meant they had been under her feet all week. She was only too glad to let them off early for 'good behaviour'.

On their way up to the caves, Dave spent all his pocket money on finding little treats to please the old woman. Not that he expected her to thank him or anything. She didn't. Maddy had spent hers on a whole roast chicken going very cheap in the supermarket. 'I don't know why we bother,' Maddy moaned, 'it seems the more alive Miss Wookey becomes, the grumpier and more ungrateful she gets.'

Dave said nothing. He so badly wanted to help the old lady to sort of make up for having let Gran down, but even he could see that things couldn't go on for much longer without some sort of sensible solution.

The two of them found Tim in the guides' office, and he took them in through a side entrance to the caves, where they could slip in and feed the old lady without being seen. As they walked down into Hester's chamber, they heard her cackling with her extremely witch-like and rather unpleasant laugh. Their blood ran cold—what on earth was she doing this time?

The three of them ran down the steps just in time to see her doing a jig on the parapet above the lake, for a group of Japanese tourists who were clicking their cameras for all they were worth. The tour guide on duty was an elderly gentleman, a Mr Bertram who only worked part time. He had passed out and sat slumped in a crumpled heap on the bottom step. It had probably been the shock of seeing the witch 'come to life'. But the visitors thought they were getting a splendid display.

As Tim approached, Hester stuck out her tongue at him. 'Wot you made me sit still for? Eh? They *like* me dance! I can't understand a word they sez, but they *like* me. I'm not sitting still any more. It's all dancin' now. I like dancin'!' And with that she resumed her display, twirling so everyone could see the pretty floral print frock she was wearing, tightly bunched up with the old belt. Her purple slippers were a bit loose, and her hat kept slipping over one eye, but she was a magnificent performer; there were no two ways about it.

One of the Japanese gentlemen turned and smiled and bowed at Tim, very politely, and congratulated him on finding such a talented actress and dancer to play the part of the witch. He asked if Tim could kindly pose with the lady, as their present guide seemed to be temporarily indisposed.

Tim was horrified, but he could do nothing else. Hester acted up terribly, insisting on sitting on Tim's knee and giving him a very smelly kiss on the cheek.

From somewhere, Bledig growled, as he always did when anyone came anywhere near his mistress. Dave tossed a handful of biscuits at the animal, who immediately started crunching noisily. Dave wasn't sure which was worse, the growling or the crunching.

Tim eased Hester off his lap and bowed to the Japanese visitors, requesting them to accompany him, as he had been sent to escort them on their tour as their main guide was… unwell. 'Do something with Miss Wookey, Maddy. I'll be back for you as soon as I can,' he whispered. 'And, Dave, I think Mr Bertram is coming round. Help him back to the main office, and tell them he took a funny turn and I've taken over.'

The old man was indeed coming to his senses as Tim led the party away, in full swing with his tales and legends. The elderly gentleman clutched his spinning head and groaned. 'I always thought the old girl was alive, but I never thought I'd *see* it,' the elderly man shook his head. 'Never in a month of Sundays.'

Dave helped the guide up the steps, praying he wouldn't turn back and see Maddy giving Hester a jolly good telling off. 'It's all right Mr Bertram,' Dave assured him. 'It's been a long day, and those shadows down there can play funny tricks with your eyes, can't they?'

But Mr Bertram was not to be put off. 'I did see her, properly this time. Not like before.'

Dave's heart missed a beat. What *had* Hester been up to? Mr Bertram continued. 'You probably think me a dotty old man, but when there's no one around she moves, you know. I swear I've seen her *knitting* lately! Of course, when I looked closer, she was only stone as usual, but I've always *felt* she was real…'

Maddy could hear no more of the conversation, because Dave led Mr Bertram away, his short, plump figure propping up the tall, thin man in a most peculiar and lopsided way. Dave's kind and reassuring voice could be heard gently mumbling as the two melted into the shadows at the top of the stairs.

Hester Wookey sat on her little space overlooking the water below as if nothing had happened, except that her flowery skirt was hitched up to show her ancient woollen smock underneath, and her hat had slipped right to one side, giving her a jaunty, even

61

clownish air. But she looked miserably pathetic and cross rather than funny. And she wouldn't move or speak to Maddy. Still as stone she sat.

'Come on, Miss Wookey, you can't sulk all day. We've bought a nice fat chicken for you.' Hester's eyes momentarily jerked towards Maddy, but immediately they flicked back to stare at the water again. 'I've bought you some chocolate.' Maddy tried again, unwrapping the bar and waving it temptingly under Hester's nose. Chocolate had become the old lady's favourite treat since she had come to life.

Still nothing.

'Oh well, if you've turned to stone again, you won't want any of these things, will you?' Maddy started to pack everything back in her bag.

Suddenly Hester snapped her gummy jaws and hissed. 'What you want then?' she demanded. 'Me to stay still or move? Make yer minds up will yer? Seems I get into trouble whatever I does. 'Snot fair, that's what I say! I don't think yez really wants me alive, do yez?'

Maddy sighed. 'Miss Wookey, we do want you alive. Dave and I were the ones who wished it from the wizard at the fairground place. But you're making it really difficult. Sometimes you can dance, and sing too if you want—that's when there's no one here. The rest of the time we need you to take your new clothes off and sit quite still, just as you used to.'

Hester gathered her pretty dress around her and looked primly shocked. 'I'm not takin' me clothes off! Not for you nor nobody!'

Maddy shook her head. 'Not *all* your clothes, Miss Wookey—just your pretties. We are trying to think of a way of sorting this out, but we're at a loss, and it's taking a long time. You see,' she added thoughtfully, 'when we wished for you to come alive, we didn't really expect it to happen.'

The old lady hung her head and let a tear roll down her exceptionally long and crooked nose. Then she sniffed and wiped the tear and the snot all the way up the sleeve of her nice new dress. Maddy took out a tissue and offered it to Hester. The crone looked at the tissue and picked it up, licked it, held it to the light and poked at it until it was in shreds. Then she pushed it into her mouth and tried chewing it. Then she spat it out.

It was hard for Maddy not to laugh. 'No, Miss Wookey, you don't eat it… try blowing your nose, then you'll feel better.'

'Do *wot* to me nose?' Hester looked alarmed.

'Blow it—you know, breathe hard outwards through your nose so all the snot comes out, and you wipe it away with the tissue.' She held out a fresh one. Hester looked at it critically. 'Don't like the sound of *that*. What do you do with the snot then? Save it till later when you be a bit peckish?'

'*NO* Miss Wookey!' Maddy was getting quite exasperated. She sat hunched on the low wall next to the old lady and found herself saying, 'It's true that sometimes I wish you hadn't come alive. It was a stupid thing for us to have wished. You were probably happier being stone. No one tried telling you what you could or couldn't do. You probably didn't feel things, like lonely and cold and stiff, did you?' Maddy glanced sideways at Miss Wookey. She'd had the same thoughts about her Gran when she was alone in a chilly flat.

Hester wiped her nose up her sleeve and looked disgusted. 'Huh! Wishing didn't do nuffing.' She snorted. 'It woz time for me to do sum movin' anyway,' Hester informed her. 'Sitting too long in one place makes yer bones ache. Still, you got me now. Where's that supper you said you got for me?'

Maddy passed over the plastic bag and stood up as Dave came running back. 'Mr Bertram is OK, although he's still rambling on about Miss Wookey being alive. No one believes him. They think he's gone a bit dotty in the head. I told the chief guide that Tim had taken the tour over. We'd better scram in case we get in the way of the next group.' Then he looked at Hester. 'Will you be all right Miss Wookey? We'll come and see you tomorrow, as usual.'

Hester glowered. 'No, I will NOT be all right! And wot makes you think your visits are so speshal that I waits for 'em? I might be here, I might not. I might just be bored of sitting here all alone, day after day. I might jest take meself off to see the king.' And she got up and pranced around, swinging her skirts from side to side. Then she swept a surprisingly good curtsy.

'Queen,' said Maddy, absently.

'Oh, so Mathilda won, did she? Good for 'er!' Hester looked almost happy.

'Who?'

'Queen Mathilda, you sez we'z got a Queen now.'

Dave suddenly realized that Hester Wookey still thought she was in the middle ages. He nudged Maddy and whispered, 'Stephen and Mathilda, remember? She thinks we're in the year 1100 and something!'

Maddy went cold. 'She's going to be terrified if she ever gets out of these caves, what with aeroplanes and cars and computers and everything. She'll never be able to handle money either.'

64

Hester leaned over and prodded the children in the ribs with her bony fingers. 'Wot's you two mutterin' about then, eh?'

Thankfully, Tim arrived at that moment. 'Hurry up, I can hear the next tour coming now. Bye, Miss Wookey, see you tomorrow.'

'Not if I sees you first,' the old woman muttered angrily to herself, and turned her back on them.

Too Late!

Out in the open air again, the three looked at each other. Dave gave a low whistle. 'I don't know how much more of this I can stand,' he said. This was most unlike Dave; he was always so patient and sympathetic. Now he really was at the end of his tether. 'I've spent all my money on her. I've sold some of my favourite gear just to keep her going. I'm skint.' And to emphasize the point he pulled his trouser pockets inside out. A piece of chewed gum fell out, attached to a pencil stub. And that was it. Not even a used tissue. 'She just takes and takes and takes, then moans and moans and moans! I really have had enough!'

Maddy shook her head and stared at the flagstones as she walked along. 'She's making my life a misery too.'

'Gran was never like this,' Dave said miserably.

'I suppose we both thought just 'cause Miss Wookey was a sad, lonely old lady in a cold, damp place, she'd be all loving and kind like Gran if we warmed her up a bit.' Maddy shrugged. 'But she's not even grateful!'

Tim sighed. 'You meant well, kids, but perhaps it wasn't all that well thought out, eh? We're going to have to think of something. The situation is getting serious all round, and, to be fair, it must be pretty miserable for her having woken up after several hundred years' snooze or whatever it was, and she's not allowed to move, or speak, or anything.'

Dave nodded. 'Imagine how she must feel… here's some nice clothes, but you can't wear them. We've wished you awake but you've got to be seen and not heard… I'd *hate* it, I know!'

Maddy said nothing. She did not feel like being understanding. She was cross that they now had no money, lots of trouble at school and at home, and, on top of all that, the old lady refused to be nice and kind and granny-ish. Maddy felt cheated and short-changed. After all they had been through. It really was too bad of her!

Tim dug into his overall pocket. 'Here,' he handed them £1. 'Go and have some fun at the arcades. They're open for another hour. Cheer yourselves up!' Then he went through the small gate that led the guides away to their office.

Maddy stared after him. It was a lovely, warm spring evening. The deep dell that nestled the caves and the other exhibits was gloriously green and rich and fertile. They should have felt blissfully happy and glad to be alive. Instead they were utterly miserable.

'Well, give Tim his due. He didn't say "I told you so!" Not once.' Dave tossed the £1 coin in the palm of his hand. 'Decent bloke that. Come on, let's go and have some fun and forget the old witch for a bit. But we mustn't be long,' he added, 'Mum will have tea ready soon.'

'Do you really think Miss Wookey's a witch?' Maddy trotted behind her brother as he climbed down the steps towards the water-wheel behind the paper-mill.

Dave shrugged. 'If she is, I don't think she's bad—just miserable and lonely.'

'How come you always see the best in people, Dave? She's a miserable old cow, and that's all there is to it.'

'True, but she's a lonely one, and frightened too, I bet.'

'Frightened? What of? We've been marvellous to her!' Maddy was feeling miffed. After all the TLC they'd poured out, Miss Wookey was still just a grumpy old lady, whom nobody wanted—and Maddy could see why.

'Yes, frightened! Can you imagine what it's like to be sat all alone for centuries with nothing but the bats and a few frogs for company. When someone does come and see you, it's to call you a witch and try and destroy you, or they haven't come to see you at all, but they are hiding contraband or disposing of a murdered body or something.'

Maddy shivered. 'I still don't see why she should be scared now though.'

Dave opened the door that led inside the mill. It was a shame to be going inside again on such a nice evening, but they must not be long; they'd be expected home soon. He continued with his thoughts. 'After centuries in the dark, along come men with muskets to blast the stalactites down—and without a by-your-leave as well. They were *hers* as much as anybody's. The noise must have been terrifying. Then there were banquets down there, and don't forget they used to light bales of straw to illuminate everything. Imagine the smoke! She must have wondered what was going on and whether she was next!'

Maddy followed her brother along the high balcony

inside the mill. He was stubborn. Once he'd got an idea into his head there was no budging him. But she was angry, and she was going to enjoy it for every bit it was worth. 'But what's the old bat got to be scared of now?' she persisted.

Dave stopped and turned to look his sister straight in the face. 'Just put yourself in her shoes for once. After all that, suddenly electric lights come on, people come and stare at you and poke at you, and make fun of you. You've got no way to argue or tell your side of the story... nothing. Then along we come and make a stupid wish and drag her into a world almost 1,000 years after her own, and expect her to behave nicely. I don't know about you. *I'd* be frightened.'

They went through the next set of doors to the paper-making room, where they could watch the men 'couching' the paper pulp. Dave sat down hard on one of the observation benches and stared at the men working. Silently he watched their dipping and rocking motion as they took tray after tray of cotton pulp and layered it between woollen blankets to be squeezed.

'I guess Hester Wookey's a bit like that paper really,' he said at last. 'She started out as old rags, but with a bit of patience she could become a nice piece of paper.'

'Well I'm out of patience. Bother the paper. I wish she was turned back to stone! Really I do.'

Dave looked down at the £1 coin he was clutching and then he looked at Maddy, who had flounced ahead into the fairground displays. He sighed. 'I wonder if that's the answer?' he mused.

'What now?' Maddy demanded when he caught up with her. She was feeling increasingly tired and irritable and unhappy. There was no solution. They had done something stupid. They had woken someone who was best left to sleep, and they had no way of caring for her. She felt guilty and angry.

Dave tugged at his sister's sleeve. 'C'mon Mads.'

'Where?' Maddy didn't want to move. She just wanted to stay staring at the model galloper ride and never think about anything again.

'We've got to make another wish—we've got to wish her back!'

Maddy stood wide-eyed and followed her brother. 'Do you really think you can?'

'What else can we do? We can't look after her; she'll be freaked by our world. It'd kill her if she ever came out, and she can't stay in there. Can you imagine what the newspapers and TV would make of her? That old guide, Mr Bertram, told me he thought he saw her doing her knitting, and even throwing stones at people she didn't like the look of. He didn't believe his eyes, of course, but someone will, one day. She is a danger to herself. The only way we can protect her is to turn her back to stone.'

'But do you think she wants to be turned back?'

Dave thought for a moment. 'No. I don't think she does. But what else do we do? Oh I don't know! It just seems kindest,' and he kicked a dustbin miserably.

They walked through the fairground exhibits and stood in front of the weird little automaton wizard with his little

Wishes Granted

sign. Dave twisted his coin between his fingers for a few moments. 'We'll need to get change first,' he mused. But hardly had the words left his mouth when the little automaton whirred and lifted his cap in time to the jangling music and dropped a little card into the brass tray below.

Just make your wish!

it said.

Dave stepped backwards, right onto Maddy's toe, making her squeal loudly. With trembling hands, Dave showed her what the card said. 'Sorry,' he muttered. 'It just made me jump. I didn't put any money in or anything!'

Maddy looked at the card and at the nasty-faced little automaton. 'I don't like this,' she whispered, 'I don't think this is the right thing to do, somehow.'

Dave looked at his sister, and spread his hands. 'Any other ideas? I can't think of anything, and we've got to do something now, before she runs riot!'

Maddy looked glum and lost. 'No,' she said, 'I can't think of anything. I suppose we'd better do it. It's better for everyone this way.'

Dave leaned over to the mouthpiece and said quite clearly, 'I wish the witch was stone again!'

The wizard opened and shut his little mechanical mouth. As he did so, a series of short, sharp laughs came out and the little figure rocked and shook as the tiny wooden rods and strings whirred into action. After a few seconds, the automaton doffed his pointed hat and dropped a second card into the brass tray below.

Trembling, Dave put out a hand and picked up the card. As usual, the ink was still wet. But this time the message was:

Too late

Hester Runs Riot

11

But the laughing of the little automaton did not cease when the shutter mouth stopped moving. The black glass eyes stared dully out of the wooden head as the figure came to a lopsided standstill. But the unpleasant laughter went on. Maddy and Dave felt cold and scared. What was happening? And, even worse, *who* was doing it?

Slowly, very slowly, the children turned their heads as they realized that the sound was actually coming from behind them. There was Hester Wookey, dressed in her red hat, flowery dress, green cardigan and purple slippers. She looked dreadful! Her nose almost touched her chin as she grinned and cackled, showing a vast expanse of sparsely toothed pink gums and the cavernous black hole of her mouth.

'Ooops!' muttered Dave and Maddy together as they both took a step backwards.

'I should fink so too!' Hester scowled as she took the small card out of Dave's hand. 'I can read, I can. In't I clever?' Then she tutted solemnly. 'Tryin' to get rid of me woz ya? Well I'm not goin' back there, not never, not nohow! So there!' And she pranced away among the exhibits in time to the barrel-organ music that was playing in the background.

The barrel-organ was a huge, magnificent creation complete with prettily carved ladies in short, tight-fitting velvet jackets and leggings, tapping brass bells in time to the music. The swathes of gold-and-red painted flowers gleamed in the light of a spinning reflector globe hanging from the ceiling. It was a beautiful sight. After a few minutes Hester stopped her dancing, looked bemused and walked round the back of the organ.

'Where'zem musicians?' she demanded. 'I wants a word wiv 'em!' she announced.

'What *is* she doing?' Maddy watched aghast as Dave sprang after her.

Behind, amongst all the rolls of waxed paper, carved pipes and moving parts, the old lady stood amazed, watching the endless twitching of the mechanism. For a few moments she just stared. Then she turned around slowly and watched each piece moving. 'I gits it,' she muttered, and after a few moments' tapping around the music suddenly became much louder and Hester came out, flushed and beaming. Followed by a flustered-looking Dave.

'That's better. I likes a good tune, I does! But I likes it good an' noisey. Don't know where them muzicians gorn to. Gorn 'ome an' left their music playin' all by itself. Clever though. Must be magic.' And she resumed her funny little jig.

Dave looked at Maddy in bewilderment. 'How did someone from the eleventh century find the volume control?'

Maddy shrugged and looked bewildered. 'Search me. Perhaps she is a witch after all…?' Hester took no notice of the children, and just danced as if she was really happy.

Suddenly she stopped dancing and clambered up the prettily carved front structure of the organ and stole one of the little brass bells from the wooden girl on the left. 'Hey!' Maddy shouted, 'Hey, you mustn't do that!'

Hester simply ignored her and twirled past with a wickedly twinkling eye and keeping steady time with her new toy. Faster and faster she span and jigged until the music roll ended. Again she dived around the back, and came out looking bewildered, and draped with miles of waxed organ roll paper, pierced with its strange, endless patterns of oblong dots and dashes.

The old lady shrugged as she dropped the paper and trampled over it. 'Never mind, I woz bored with that anyhow!'

Maddy dived forward and tried to retrieve the roll, frantically attempting to rewind it, but getting in a worse tangle than even Hester had managed. 'What are we going to say if one of the staff comes along?' she wailed. Dave shrugged and looked lost. They did not have time to wonder, for Hester had spotted something else that took her fancy—huge teddy bears and ropes of glass jewellery offered as 'prizes' on the shooting gallery exhibit.

Springing lightly over the barricade, Hester helped herself to a pink fluffy bear and several necklaces before the children managed to catch up with her. 'Look, those don't belong to you. It's only an exhibit, showing how people have to shoot or throw darts or something to win prizes…' Maddy bit her lip as soon as she had spoken. It would have been better if she had just let Hester get on with her ransacking.

But it was too late. The old lady had already grasped

the idea. Immediately she dumped the toys and said, 'Why didn't yer say so then?' and picked up a rifle. 'I seen these things afore! Men used to make a big noise wiv 'em and make me pretty pointy rocks come down. I allus wanted a go, I did. But t'was the men I wanted to knock down. I liked me rocks where they woz.'

She levelled the rifle and swung it around dangerously. The children went pale and ducked and hid behind the wooden barricade. 'There won't be any ammunition in it, will there?' Dave whispered.

'Course not, it's only a display one… I hope,' Maddy replied.

Luckily, Hester couldn't make head or tail of the thing. She shook it, rattled it, peered down the barrel, and eventually found the trigger which she clicked several times, but to no effect. 'Can't win no prizis wiv that fing!' she muttered and she flung it down crossly, picked up her pink teddy and stalked away.

'Oh help, what next?' Dave was beginning to panic.

The sound of laughter made Hester run along a little corridor that bypassed the mirror maze and she found she was facing the seaside pier slot-machines. Quietly she crept up behind three small children and watched as they operated the one-armed bandits, skilfully managing to win back a few coppers almost every time.

'My turn,' she announced, and pushed herself between the children just as the youngest little girl had put in her last penny. Hester gripped the heavy metal handle of the one-armed bandit and tugged it down with a tremendous jerk.

'Hey!' the boy challenged. 'That was my sister's last penny! Shove off, you!'

But Hester Wookey took no notice at all. She just cackled with glee as the jackpot came up and a seemingly endless stream of pennies gushed out. Hester flung the pink bear aside and took off her beloved red hat to catch the coins.

Indignant, the children tried to tug the hat back, tipping coins all over the floor. 'Oi! That was *our* money!' they bellowed, outraged.

'But *I* pulled the handle!' Hester grinned, tugging the hair of the little girl she had robbed as she ran away.

'We've been mugged by an old lady!' the boy bellowed, but for some reason there was no attendant in the booth where money was changed. Dave ran up and pressed the £1 coin Tim had given them into the boy's hand. 'There, sorry about our granny; she's a bit cuckoo!' and he tapped his head meaningfully.

Maddy retrieved Hester's discarded pink teddy and pressed it into the arms of the snivelling girl. 'Here, have this; you'll have more fun with it than she will!' The little girl beamed a smile and wiped her nose on the back of the teddy's head.

Satisfied, the boy took his little sisters by the hand and glared back at Hester, who was feeding their winnings into another fruit machine. 'We're off!' he said. 'She oughta be put away, she ought!' and ran towards the exit.

Maddy looked at her watch. 'This is getting serious, Dave. We're the only people in the place, and it's all going to be locked up at any moment!'

'So are we if it goes on like this!' Dave moaned, pointing at Hester, who was playing on a bagatelle, flicking the levers far too hard and spinning the tiny silver balls so fast that they almost broke the glass on the front. Then, when Hester did not win, she began to thump the machines and rock them, kicking and swearing in a most unladylike way. 'Me money's all gorn. I wants it back I does!'

Maddy whispered to Dave, 'I'll try and distract her while you find a member of staff. This is getting ridiculous!' Then she went over to Hester and held out her hand to her. 'Come and look at the pretty pictures, Miss Wookey; you'll like these!'

Hester grabbed Maddy's hand in her filthy claw and trotted after her, almost obediently. 'So far, so good,' Maddy thought to herself. If only I can keep this up just a little longer...' She led the old lady over to the photographer's studio, where Maddy had posed as 'Calamity Jane' with her birthday money.

Hester was astounded at the pictures. At first she could not believe that anyone could draw that well. Then she thought people had been caught by spells and squashed up behind the glass. Next she tried to pick the front off one portrait to see how the people had managed to get made so small and flat. Maddy took her over to the camera, set up ready for the next day, and tried to explain how it worked, and how a photograph was made.

Fairly predictably, Hester then tried to open the back of the big plate camera, which Maddy thought might contain people's undeveloped pictures. She could see another catastrophe approaching fast, when suddenly Hester's eye was caught by the racks of costumes hanging up ready for use. The old lady pushed the camera tripod over and darted off in the direction of the hundreds of 'pretties'.

Her newly developed passion for clothes was all-consuming. Within two bounds Hester had crossed the room and was pulling dresses off their hangers, holding them up, and dropping them on the floor. Frantically, Maddy followed behind, trying to pick things up and re-hang them before they got too trampled.

But no matter how fast she worked, Hester worked faster, and soon the floor was a sea of Victorian frills and laces, hats, bonnets, parasols, huge wire hoops for skirts and discarded horsehair bustles.

'Stop, *please*, Miss Wookey; we're going to get into terrible trouble! Please stop!' Maddy begged, close to tears.

Hester just laughed and held up a pretty pink dress trimmed with soft white lace all around the neck.

'This'll do!' she announced. 'I'll be as pretty as one of 'em pictures in this!' and she started to tug at her floral print dress. Within seconds she was standing in her ancient woollen smock, struggling to pull the pink taffeta on over it. Maddy could do nothing to stop her, so she began to help the old lady with the fastenings. 'Perhaps, if she's happy with the dress, she might give up and calm down,' Maddy thought. 'Then we might be able to do something with her.'

But it was not to be.

Hester Wookey, as usual, had her own ideas. She sat down hard in the magnificent carved chair in front of the camera. 'I wants me picture took!' she demanded. 'Pretty-like, mind you!'

Frantic with worry, Maddy obediently took the cover off the camera and peered through the view-finder. What she saw made her want to laugh, despite the fact that she was so close to tears.

Hester Wookey was primly posed in a pretty pink taffeta dress, but still wearing her red hat and purple slippers with bits of ancient woollen smock poking out around the neck and under the hem!

'Wouldn't you like a prettier hat, Miss Wookey?' she ventured. 'One that matches the dress, maybe?'

'What's wrong wiv this one?' Hester glowered. ''Urry up or I'll turn youz into a frog or summat rather slimy and very nasty!' Then she resumed her pose, looking unbelievably prim.

Maddy was fairly convinced that Hester had no spells at all, and that she was all wind and noise. But she did as she was told, just to please her. Anything, *anything* just to get out of here!

Just as the flash fired, Dave came back, looking extremely miserable. 'There's absolutely no one around,' he said. 'And, what's worse, we're locked in!'

Mirror Maze

12

'Locked in!' Maddy went quite white. 'There must be a phone or something… We'll have to look.'

Dave shook his head. 'The main office door is locked; I tried. There's got to be some sort of alarm we can set off. We'll just have to keep her as amused as possible while we keep looking. What *is* she up to now?'

Hester Wookey had discovered the maze of mirrors. She was standing with both her grimy hands on her hips, wagging her head from side to side in the first mirror, talking to her reflection.

Suddenly she pulled back her fist and thumped at the glass. Thankfully it didn't break, but it did make her cry. Maddy ran over and tried to pat and soothe Hester's bony hand.

'Nasty lady there; she sez wot I sez. She's very rude!' Hester moaned. 'Not nice. She's wearin' the same pretty dress as me too, an' won't take it off. I told 'er it's *my* dress, but she don't believe me. I'll hit her if she don't give it back. Where's that big stick thing that bangs fings? I'll hit her wiv that.' And she waved her fist threateningly at herself.

Dave put a reassuring hand on Hester's arm. 'No, Miss Wookey, calm down. That lady is you. This is a mirror.'

Hester looked back into the glass, head on one side, then on the other. 'Can't be. She's an ugly bint an' I bain't. I'm beautiful!'

Maddy tried this time. 'It is a mirror, Miss Wookey. It's ever so polished glass, like silver, and you see yourself in it. Look…' and she stood close to Hester so the old lady could see the shared reflection. Hester glowered at the image of the short, plump girl in a blue shirt and jeans and compared it with the real person standing next to her… 'And here's Dave, look.'

Hester looked at the children's reflections again, and then at herself once more. 'Well, someone's put a spell on it, that's all I can say. I'll go and find a mirror that's not all befuddled with spells n' stuff…' And with that she stepped into the maze, peering at all the mirrors in turn. After a few minutes, she became less concerned about how ugly she looked, and more interested in how pretty her dress was. She found if she stood in front of one mirror, and swung her silky pink skirt, at least four Hesters danced for her. Soon the old lady was cackling and cooing as happy as anything.

'If she stays like that for a few minutes, we've got a chance,' Dave whispered. But before either of them could move, Hester had whooped for joy and plunged further into the maze, laughing with glee at the ever-increasing number of images of her pretty dress reflected all around. 'This be fun!' she squealed as she disappeared.

'We'd better follow her; it can be pretty frightening in there. It's sort of spooky when you can't find your way out.' Maddy plunged reluctantly between the mirrors, with Dave right behind her.

'I'm hopeless at this,' Dave moaned. 'I always end

up bashing my nose on the glass in front when I think I'm stepping somewhere, only I'm not.'

'Easy,' Maddy retorted. 'Look straight ahead. Where there's no reflection of yourself in front, that means there's no mirror, so you can go that way. Look, you can even run through…' And with that she pranced ahead, not waiting for her brother.

Soon Dave was standing all alone, facing the maze nervously, only hearing the faint sounds of Hester's cackling laugh and Maddy calling after the wayward old lady. He shrugged, and plunged between the huge glass panels.

At first, everything went very smoothly—turn, turn, step. He caught a glimpse of a shiny pink taffeta skirt ahead, but when he stepped that way he hit his nose on the glass. He must have glimpsed Hester reflected from behind. He turned and found he was only staring at his own round, pink freckled face. He was shocked to see how tired and worried he looked. He patted the glass. 'Don't worry old chum,' he said softly to his image, 'we'll get out of this. She's not really a witch, and they'll find us in the morning.' As he looked around he realized he had walked right out of the mirrors, and was standing at another entrance.

Suddenly he jumped as music started next to his ear. Without realizing it, he had been standing next to a walled pool. As he turned to look, a fountain sprang into life, shooting spouts of brightly lit water high into the air, in time to the music.

Next second, Hester Wookey was there, peering in anger and amazement at the fountain. Millions of tiny coloured lights shining into the water fascinated her, and when she found she couldn't grab them with her

82

fingers, she hitched up her skirt and tried to clamber in, fully dressed, purple, flowered slippers and all.

Dave grabbed hold of her arm and tried to hold her back.

'Maddy!' he bawled. 'Help!'

But it was too late. Hester was already waddling through the water, getting thoroughly drenched as she groped around in the bottom, sticking her fingers in the fountain spouts.

'Pixies! It gotta be them wretched pixies! Or maybe it's a will-o'-the-wisp from outta them marshes. Either way I'll gettem!'

'What's she talking about?' Maddy asked, as she came puffing up to the fountain.

'I think she thinks they're those funny little marsh lights that lead people astray in bogs and stuff,' Dave answered. 'You know, the flames caused by rotting vegetation giving off methane gas. They used to think they were spirits or pixies in olden days.'

Maddy looked round the back of the pool and found a switch. 'Well let's make them go away, or we'll never get her out,' she said as she flipped the little lever to 'off'.

Hester looked around, astonished as the lights went out and the music stopped all at the same moment. 'Where're they gorn?' she asked, angry that the pixies had evaded her.

Maddy pointed to the switch. 'It's only a trick,' she assured the old lady. 'They weren't real. Now let's get you dry and find some way out of here.'

But Hester was having none of it. 'Youz not taking me pretties away. Oh no youz not. I'm orf!' and with that she clambered out of the water and disappeared into the maze again. Dave and Maddy ran after her, but the slipperiness of her wet clothes meant they could not catch hold of her properly. Again and again she evaded them. She seemed to have a real knack of finding her way through the maze without banging her head and nose like the children did. Dave caught hold of the tail of Maddy's shirt to keep from being separated from her, but even then they often found themselves staring at more mirrors rather than at each other.

Suddenly, Maddy stopped and stood stock-still, Dave bumped hard into the back of her. 'Ouch!' she complained. 'Watch it!'

'What did you stop like that for?'

'I want to get my bearings.'

'Your what?'

'My bearings; we've lost her!'

'No we haven't—look!' and as Dave pointed, a whisk of pink taffeta fluttered past them and the chase was on again.

Maddy suddenly realized that the witch's feet were wet. 'Look, if we follow the footmarks we'll catch her. She's leaving a watery trail everywhere she goes.'

So, keeping their heads down, the two set off again. But after a few moments, Maddy stopped dead again. This time Dave managed not to collide with her. 'What now? There're her foot marks; we must be behind her.'

'In theory, yes. But look, we've been here before; there's a screwed up chewing-gum wrapper next to her footprint. I've seen it before. I'm certain she's tricked us!'

Hester's cackling laughter suddenly rattled in from nowhere. 'Can't catch me!' she called.

'Where is she?' demanded Maddy crossly. 'She really is a pain. I'm so tired and I want to go home. I've had enough. I wish she'd stop being silly so we can find a way out.'

'Me too,' said Dave, as picked up the chewing-gum wrapper and looked at it. 'And I've just had an idea to help us catch her. Let's set off following the footprints again, and I'll tear this bit of paper into tiny pieces and drop bits as we go. Then we'll soon see whether we're going round in circles or not.'

So they set off again, but each time they stepped past a mirror, Dave dropped a fragment of paper. It only took a minute or two before they were definitely back where they'd begun. 'Bother!' Dave stamped his foot. 'Have you got any more paper, Mads?'

She shook her head. 'Haven't you? Your pockets are always bulging with gunge.'

'No. Mum made me empty everything out this morning… But what I can't work out is how we can be going round in circles, I mean we're following her footsteps, so she's either right behind us, or we're caught in some sort of a mirror trap.'

The thought made them both go cold. Slowly they both turned and looked over their shoulders, but they were alone. They could only see themselves reflected a million times into infinity in every direction.

Maddy would not accept defeat. 'Or, she could have jumped of course. Look, she went this way…' She led off after the rapidly drying footsteps again, 'and when you get to this point, there's no reflection of yourself in *two* directions. I reckon when she saw her footprints had caught up with themselves she just jumped the other way to mislead us.'

'She may be hundreds of years old, but she's mighty clever, I'll give her that,' muttered Dave as he ran after Maddy, who had disappeared down the other glassy lane.

A Magical Ride

As usual, Hester Wookey was ahead of them. She had run back into the hall with the fairground exhibits and had sat astride a little wooden cockerel 'galloper', painted in glossy gold with a glowing scarlet tail and comb, with gorgeous deep-turquoise feathers richly bunched all around the throat.

Hester was rocking to and fro on the little carved creature, until it creaked painfully on its twisted brass pole. She was hitting the poor thing very hard with the flat of her hand, leaving grimy smears all over the magnificently painted neck feathers.

'Quick,' called Dave, 'we must stop her! She'll break it in a minute!'

'Either that or she'll take off!' squealed Maddy as she leaped forward, followed closely by Dave.

But Hester was too fast for them. She slid off the cockerel onto the other side and ran over to the little wishing wizard. Then, before the twins could stop her, she had produced an old penny from the lining of her beloved red hat, and pushed it into the slot.

'I wish theze fings could fly!' she cackled. 'I alluz wanted to fly!' she added as she leaped back onto the poor cockerel. The little automaton had scarcely begun to wheeze into life before the huge carved bird

87

began to scratch itself and stretch its wooden wings. As the old lady slid into place on its back, the brass pole that supported it on the display shook loose and fell off with a clatter, leaving the animal free for the first time since it was made. It threw back its head and crowed so loudly and gleefully that they all jumped.

Suddenly it was off, strutting around the display hall, with the old lady gripping its feathers, holding on with a grim determination.

The twins looked at each other, then began to give chase.

As the twins ran past the gallopers, two great carved naiads stepped down from where they had been holding the galloper canopy with Neptune. They hooked the brightly coloured canvas up to the ceiling so Neptune himself could lower his thickly muscled back and follow his daughters, the spirits of the rivers and streams. The wonderful carved figures stretched out their long, strong arms and beckoned to the children. 'Come, jump onto a galloper quickly! We must catch her!'

Without stopping to wonder *how* they would catch her, Maddy and Dave hopped onto a pair of carved animals. Maddy's was a white mare wearing a gleaming blue bridle and purple saddle, with huge, brown eyes and a cream-coloured muzzle. Dave's was a fiery zebra with a blood-red saddle and bridle, stamping and raring to go.

Maddy thought how odd it felt to be seated on something which was still definitely wooden, but yet at the same time so alive and supple of limb. She leaned forward and stroked the animal's neck. It snickered with pleasure as it stamped the ground and shook itself free of its great pole. With great, smooth strides, the white pony jumped down and began to pace its way around the hall, moving with a lithe grace that would have been delightful in a real animal.

Maddy looked back at Dave, whose zebra had just shaken itself free of its pole. The creature was rearing and neighing with the delight of freedom.

'Quick, quick!' urged the first naiad, who had already stepped through the wall of oddly twisted crazy mirrors as if they were no more substantial than a thin curtain of water. Beyond, as she held the soft reflections back for the children to pass through, Maddy and Dave could see the open hillside.

They hesitated, holding their mounts back by their painted leather harnesses. The mirrors made everything look so strange that they began to feel dizzy as they watched. The world seemed to be swimming around them. Was it all real?

Just then, the second naiad, as tall and graceful as the first, ran ahead, holding the hand of her father Neptune. They looked down at the children kindly, their gold paint gleaming in the last rays of the spring sunset. 'Come on, it's quite safe. Come and ride while we run!'

They beckoned to the children and then turned to run with huge, swift strides up the Mendip hillside to the wild spaces beyond. Gone were the houses and the paper-mill. The river Axe lay far below them, glistening silver in the dark evening shadows that were swiftly engulfing everything.

The heavy hoof beats of the children's mounts had ceased, and the children realized with a thud of fear that they were *flying*. Their fairground gallopers were treading air and wind, following the huge, mythical figures as they ran ahead, their feet touching nothing. The naiads' loose, lovely clothes flapped in the wind as they floated up out of the valley.

On the top of the hill, everything was wild and bare. The wind whistled and howled as night fell and the horse and zebra landed on the soft, springy turf. They almost bounced as they leaped and ran with heart-bursting joy across the hilltop. Ahead of the twins ran the great wooden figures of Neptune and his daughters, with the smooth grace of trained athletes, mile after mile. The wild wind blew in their faces, and tossed their golden locks of hair back from their finely carved faces. They were so alive—much more alive than real people, if that were possible!

The carved figures laughed as they ran, but it was not Hester's mean-minded laughter; it was real hilarity. But it was also the sound of running waves, great breakers and tiny streams, all rolling and sounding at once, as though all the waters in the world were flowing together, celebrating creation.

Maddy and Dave found the sound infectious, and they began laughing too. They soon found they were riding properly, not just a frantic clinging-on as when they had first mounted their fairground rides. Now they had become one with their mounts.

They gripped with their knees and leaned forward just enough to give their animals the right balance. They were away, feeling all the weariness and worry of the past weeks lifting away from them as they galloped.

Despite the newly fallen dark, the moon shone brightly, cloaking everything in a pure silver light. The stars shone as bright as pinpricks in the clear, almost crystal night around them. High above them, the Great Bear looked down on the chase with mild interest.

Way ahead was Hester Wookey on her great golden cockerel, but the children had almost forgotten her with the exhilaration of the ride. If only they could ride like that for ever… That was pure joy; that must be heaven!

Fairly predictably it was Dave who thought of Hester first. 'I wonder if the old lady is enjoying *her* ride? I hope she's all right, but she *did* wish for it!' he bellowed across to Maddy. The wind snatched the words from his mouth, and he had to yell it several times before his sister caught the drift of what he was saying.

Frantically they waved and hallooed until one of the naiads slowed down to run between the twins. She looked like a beautiful girl of about twenty, dressed in a long, loose robe like the ancient Romans might have worn. Her eyes sparkled and laughed. Every moment of the run seemed to be sheer joy to her as well.

'Where's Miss Wookey? Is she all right?' Dave managed to communicate at last. The Naiad stretched out a roundly carved arm, and pointed ahead. 'Not far now,' she sang in a delicious, rippling, watery voice that was thrilling to hear. 'We will go ahead to make sure she doesn't come to harm!' Then she sprinted on ahead to run beside her father and sister.

In truth, Maddy did not want to find Hester. She wanted the ride to go on and on for ever. What was the point of capturing her? She would only shout and swear at them, calling them names and demanding more and more of everything. She had half a mind to keep on riding, but what if her horse turned back to wood all the way out here on the wild Mendips, with not even a farm in sight? But one thing did intrigue her; when the naiad spoke, she was certain she had heard that voice before—and that laugh, but when? Where?

Suddenly they found they were slowing down. The wind blew more gently and had ceased its whistle. Their hair ceased to lash their faces and the horses slackened their pace and moved more gently. They were in the middle of a strange place, where the land was cut away in deep channels making strange, black shadowy shapes below. Ahead, Hester and the naiads were standing on what could only be called an 'island' of rock and grass with deep channels all around. They appeared to be standing in the middle of what once must have been quarries or shallow mines. Neptune had captured the cockerel and had calmed it. Slowly the children's mounts came alongside and stopped on this little fastness. Neptune lifted the children down, his great curling beard brushing their faces softly as he picked them up in his strong arms. Their legs turned to jelly as they stood on the firm ground again. There was the Witch of Wookey Hole, captured in the gentle but very firm arms of the naiads who stood either side, holding each of the old lady's hands.

She and the children were face to face at last. What could they possibly have to say to each other now?

The Strongest Wish

14

The children looked at Hester Wookey. She was just a lonely, shrivelled old lady. Cold and frightened, she shivered between the tall, magnificent naiads who had captured her so gently.

The naiads calmed the cockerel and undid the bridles of the zebra and the mare so that they could graze. Meanwhile, Neptune turned to Hester and glared at her. 'So,' he said, prodding her a little with the blunt end of his trident, 'You have lead us all a merry dance, although I cannot deny I was glad of the exercise. We are all a little fed up with you, Miss Hester Wookey. You sat in your cave so long, sulking and refusing to speak to us, we'd almost decided you had turned to stone all the way through.

'But now you've come back with a vengeance. If anything, you are even more cross and miserable and ungrateful than you were before! I'm beginning to be sorry I allowed my daughters to hide you inside that stalagmite, and I'm certainly regretting helping you to come back to life!' His voice was rolling and deep, like water heaving in a narrow place, making a low, bell-like chiming sound. It made the children thrill with delight to hear it. But they did not understand what he was talking about at all.

Hester glowered back at the heavily carved figure that towered above her. She looked up and up to see his wide, ancient face, kind but stern under its richly flowing beard.

'Why shouldn't I come back to life then? I got every right to a bit of air, same as you. More so, cause I'm human, not like you lot; youz just myfical. Youz bain't real!'

Neptune gave the old lady another slight prod. 'We're real, all right, and we've been listening to you moaning and muttering to yourself for centuries. All we got for the help we gave you was the sulks! We've looked after you as we swam in the waters of the river, and flowed through the lake at your feet. We've watched over you for all these years. We've seen everything.'

'Bain't got nuffin' to hide!' she muttered sulkily.

'We tried to cheer you up by talking and singing to you, as our waters flowed past and as the naiads played in the lake. But you wouldn't listen. You were so wrapped up in your own misery and self pity, you couldn't be bothered with anyone else.' The King of the Sea looked genuinely concerned and sad as he stood towering over the frail old woman. Dave and Maddy could see he really did care for her.

Hester sneered up at Neptune. 'Wot I gotta be 'appy about then, eh? No one loved me, no one ever wanted me, I had stones thrown at me all me life, so I turned into one meself. Everyone spat at me an' told me I was an old witch, so I let 'em fink so. Kept 'em away from me, din' it?'

Neptune tugged his brows together and glowered, looking so storm-like everyone expected thunder and went goose-pimply. He pointed his enormous hand at Hester. 'You were meant to bring people happiness with your great beauty and your gift of dancing. You were born to help people celebrate creation, and what did you do with it? You grew mean and angry and threw away everything you had!'

Hester leaned forward and bit Neptune's finger as she tried to duck away from her captors. 'Fat lot you know about it! You being myfical an' all. It's all right for you lot. You got it good, 'in't yer? Even if youz was real, you'd be gods and stuff an' everybody finks youz wonderful and t'int fair. So there! An' wot youz doing here anyway? Neptune belongs in the sea—everyone knows that!' and she crossed her arms and turned her back extremely rudely.

Neptune scowled at his bitten finger, which really hurt him; Hester had sliced it quite badly with one of her few remaining teeth.

Then one of the naiads knelt down so she could look the old lady in the eyes and hold her hand. 'Neptune is here because the seas and rivers belong together. We are always flowing into each other. We do everything together. But most importantly we *are* real. People think we're mythical because they don't *see* us. But the rivers and seas are alive, although in this age we are dying a bit more every day because of the pollution humans throw into our waters. Maybe they wouldn't if they knew about how very alive we are. It's a bit like the way people used to treat you; they used to pelt you with stones and rubbish because they didn't understand you.

'But, despite the fact we are being destroyed, we all still have a duty to bring life wherever we can with our water and our laughter and our beauty. Perhaps one day people will learn. We just have to keep helping people understand what they are doing to us.

'But until then there's no room for hate. Where we can we keep bringing life. That's the way we were made to be. So were you! It was because we understood how you must be feeling that we lulled you to sleep with our songs, and covered you with stone so you would be safe until you felt strong enough to try to come to life again.'

Hester wriggled away from the kindly naiad and crossed her arms even more closely over her chest, hugging herself and keeping everyone at bay with nasty looks. 'There you go again. T'wasn't *you* who turned me to stone, t'was me own idea—I'm a witch, bain't I? So there!' She pulled her neck down so her chin sank hard into her bony chest.

Maddy and Dave looked at each other. Poor old lady. They knew what it was like to be teased. The only people who weren't 'got at' at their school were the bullies themselves. Everyone else was plagued by someone, either because they were too fat or too thin, or they had funny hair or a peculiar name. Dave went and put his arm around Hester and gave her a hug; even though she was smelly and nasty, he felt for her.

Maddy took one of the old lady's hands. It was cold, cold as stone.

'I wish we had the wishing wizard here to make another wish!' she said suddenly.

At this the second naiad laughed, tossing her wild, golden hair in the silver moonlight. 'Him? He only made mischief. He was made by an evil-minded little man who liked scaring people. None of the things you *really* wished for came from him.'

Dave was lost. 'So how did all those wishes come true? How did he know how to answer everything we asked for?'

'It's all tricks and deception. The only things that made anything happen were your care and love for a lost old lady, together with Hester's own will to come to life again. We helped a bit, and we woke the fairground gallopers of course. It's the magic of life and love that makes things happen. Not the wishing-wizard.'

Maddy thought about all the wishes they had made. The worst one they had made was wishing the witch back to stone. She could see now that no one had a right to do that. Hester wanted to live, so she deserved the chance to get it right this time. *Everyone* needed lots of second chances and new beginnings, however bad they'd been.

She stroked the old lady's thin hands. They were still cold, just like her Granny's used to be. '"Cold hands, warm heart," Granny used to say,' she said out loud.

'Got it! That's the wish we need!' Dave suggested.

'What do you mean?' Maddy was lost.

'Cold hands, warm *heart*! Don't you see?'

Maddy shook her head, bemused.

Dave went on. 'But perhaps we ought to make it stronger than a common or garden wish this time.'

'How do you mean?' Maddy was beginning to get cold herself, standing there on a Mendip hillside after dark. Hester was shivering badly too. She had been at a steady temperature of eleven degrees for the last 900 or so years. They had to do something before they all froze.

Dave held Hester's hands and closed his eyes. 'This is the strongest wish in the world,' he said out loud. 'Please God, can Hester Wookey have a warm heart?'

Trying to Tell the Truth

Whether they rode back on the galloper horses or whether they never left the fairground exhibition at all they never knew. But the children found themselves back, riding on an ancient merry-go-round, quite dizzy from the ride. Dave was astride a zebra with a red saddle and Maddy was riding a white pony.

Barrel-organ music was just fading as the galloper rides were slowly coming to a standstill, rising and falling on their gleaming, twisted poles. Between the children was a very wooden-looking carved cockerel, bearing a shivering little wren of an old lady in a damp pink dress, crying her eyes out as she clung to the creature's neck feathers.

Maddy turned to look back at the great statues of Neptune and his naiad daughters, who stood holding the canopy of the ride, as stiff and unmoving as the day they were carved and gilded.

As she stared at them and let the images of the evening slide across her mind, Maddy suddenly realized where she had heard the naiad's gentle voice before. It was the wonderful sound she had heard in the whirlpool cavern; the voice which had spoken when she had thrown her necklace into the river to try to make her wish come true. Scared, but at the same time hoping she was right as well, Maddy turned her head further to see the water-spirit's delicately carved neck. And there, under the gentle, smiling wooden face was Maddy's thread of pink corals.

Almost imperceptibly the naiad smiled and nodded, touching the knobbly beads with her fingertips. 'Thank you,' she whispered softly. 'That was a lovely gift.'

Suddenly, the twins realized they could smell burning. They slid from their mounts and looked around urgently. Smoke was coming from the little automaton wizard!

'The electric light at the back must have shorted!' Dave yelped. 'Quick! Where are the fire extinguishers?'

'No time!' Maddy sprang to her feet. 'Get out, get the fire brigade out! That's the rule. We daren't risk getting trapped in here with Miss Wookey—she'll never make it once the fumes take hold!'

And, sure enough, small, golden-orange flames were beginning to lick up the back of the wizard's display case in a very frightening way. As the case and its contents were very old, there was no poisonous plastic to burn, but the smell of the dusty, woody smoke was already beginning to make them cough.

Hearts pounding, the children tugged the dazed Miss Wookey down from the golden cockerel and half led, half carried her towards the exit. She was not heavy, and she no longer struggled and fought. The corridor seemed endless. In reality it wasn't very far, but the terror of the smoke and flames, which must surely catch everything else in the display alight, made every step seem to take forever. The little old iron turnstile at the exit was the biggest problem. Not because it was difficult to get through, but because Hester was fascinated by it. She kept going round and round and wouldn't come away from it. She just could not grasp the danger they were in. In the end, Dave had to climb back over the barrier and push the old lady through, while Maddy gripped her thin hands and pulled her forwards, preventing her from going round a fourth time.

Suddenly and fiercely, the alarms set off, deafening the children and Miss Wookey with an urgent, persistent screech which they could barely stand. Then, to add misery to misery, they were now getting drenched as well because the sprinkler system kicked in, dousing everything in ice-cold water.

By the time they reached the main entrance, Maddy had already worked out that if they stood on a chair and hit the glass with a flower vase from the 'enquiries' desk, they could probably get themselves out. But whether Hester could manage the climb up to the tiny paned windows, or the drop down the other side, she did not know. They would have to try and persuade her to lower herself and hang by her hands before dropping to the ground. Maddy bit her lip as she thought. This was going to be *impossible*!

Meanwhile, Dave made Hester sit in a heap behind the desk, tucking her head down between her bony knees. He told her to keep her face as close to the floor as possible, so that her nose would be below the smoke. Then he took turns with Maddy to smash at the glass. But the vase was weaker than the window and shattered in his hands.

The minutes ticked by. There was nothing they

could do. They were trapped! The twins looked at each other in horror.

The sprinklers were still pouring water, but there was no smell of smoke. 'Perhaps the fire's out,' Maddy suggested hopefully.

'Could be, but we all need to get out, let's face it. If we aren't roasted alive it looks like we'll drown.'

Just then a clattering at the door made them jump out of their skins. Then the handles moved, and in walked two black-clad fire officers, hoses in hand and breathing gear on their backs.

'Thank goodness,' Maddy muttered as she was scooped up into strong, safe arms and carried outside, 'there must have been a direct alarm to the fire station.'

Back home, wrapped in blankets and clutching mugs of hot chocolate, there seemed so much to say, but no one could hear a word because everyone was talking at once.

The twins' parents, had, of course, been frantically worried when the children had not returned from visiting the caves. The police had been called and were about to enter the caves to look for them when the fire alarms had been set off. The police had called the fire brigade and the children had been found very quickly after that.

But Maddy and Dave's story about Miss Wookey was the difficult bit for all the adults to cope with. They did not seem to be able to grasp the truth. They gleaned that the twins had found a very elderly lady wandering around the caves on her own, and she had proved very difficult to get out as she had gone a bit potty in the displays. They had all got locked in, and the fire had been an accidental short in electrical equipment. Everyone was happy with that explanation, at least until morning.

'They'll soon find out the truth,' Maddy groaned. 'Why is the truth so difficult for adults to understand? They get cross when we don't tell the truth, then they get even crosser if we do!'

'You said it!' Dave sighed. 'If I know Mum and Dad, they'll be up half the night worrying and talking it all over. We'll get treble-grounded and goodness knows what else. In the morning they'll sit us down and very *nicely* tell us they don't believe us, and we'll have to start with the explanations all over again!'

Mum made up a bed for Miss Wookey on the settee. But the strange visitor seemed more interested in watching the tropical fish swimming round and round in the aquarium. Occasionally she put her hand into the water and tried to grab a few of the little guppies.

Maddy went and made some sardines on toast and put the plate on Hester's lap. 'Try these, Miss Wookey. They taste much better than the live ones. Less bones to crunch.'

'But I likes the crunchy bones! Them's the best bit!' Hester complained as she rammed slice after slice of tomatoey, sardiney toast into her mouth, shoving the stray bits in with her grubby fingers. 'Give us some of that tea stuff will yer?' Hester smiled charmingly as she wiped her fingers on the remains of the pink taffeta dress.

Dad went into the kitchen and put cups out while Maddy made the tea. 'Mum and I are a bit nervous about having her in the house at all, to be honest. But, poor old dear, she seems so frail, and I can see what

Dave means; she does have something like Gran about her—sort of lost and lonely, despite her mischief.'

Dad brought the tea in, put it down on the coffee table and smiled. 'Sleep well, Miss Wookey. We'll have another talk in the morning and see if we can help you find somewhere nice to live.'

Dave hoped Mum and Dad wouldn't offer the old woman a home, like they ought to have done for Gran. Hester *was* impossible. She would wreck everything within a couple of days. They just couldn't do it. Dad and Mum both had jobs, and Maddy and Dave had to go to school—although they felt as if they hadn't seen much of it lately.

Mum persuaded Hester to lie still in bed at last. The old lady had fallen asleep almost immediately, and was snoring loudly. 'She could do with a bath, for a start,' Mum said, holding her nose as she tiptoed past her guest. 'I couldn't persuade her to even go into the bathroom. She looks as if she hasn't washed for a hundred years!'

Dave and Maddy cleaned their teeth and left their bedroom doors ajar so they could hear as much as they possibly could from downstairs.

The twins could hear Hester's snores loud and clear from their bedrooms. Mum came up and tucked them in. She sat on the end of Maddy's bed, so she could see into Dave's room as well. 'We'll have to get a social worker in to see her tomorrow,' Mum whispered. 'The poor old dear has no idea where she is… I think she's escaped from somewhere, but no doubt she's harmless enough.'

'I wouldn't be so sure,' Dave muttered as he drifted off to sleep.

In the middle of the night, the whole house was woken by the television blaring very loudly.

Within minutes, everyone was awake, watching aghast as Hester Wookey zoomed through all the television channels as fast as she could, with the volume turned up as loud as it would go. 'I'm lookin' for a good tune,' she grumbled. 'There bain't no tunes on this wretched thing!' and she started hitting the remote control very hard on the top of the telly.

'Just a mo,' Maddy rummaged through a cupboard until she found a CD with lively dance music on.

'That's a bit loud,' Dad said as he wrestled the remote from Hester's vice-like fingers.

'She won't have it any quieter,' Dave assured him.

'Give her the earphones, for crying out loud!' Dad bellowed as he went to put the kettle on.

Mum was already on the phone to the duty social worker. 'Yes, I *know* it's three o'clock in the morning, but this is an emergency. You've got to come and get her or there'll be a murder before morning,' Mum assured the bemused lady on the other end of the phone.

The children went to see Hester the following day in the local home for elderly people. The matron was no bigger than Hester herself, but had a will of iron, and soon had the old lady bathed (the first one of her life), hair washed, cut and combed, nails trimmed, and her remaining teeth cleaned.

In the morning the police arrived. They wanted the children to help get Hester's version of the events of the previous night. They certainly hadn't got very far with her on their own.

At first, when they were shown into the lounge by

matron, they all looked around, bemused. There was no Hester Wookey. Then the matron smiled, took Maddy's arm and steered her towards a corner of the room where a respectable-looking lady sat in a comfy chair, bouncing up and down to music on earphones, blissfully unaware of the visitors.

Matron came and unhooked the earphones and switched the cassette player off. 'You've got visitors, Miss Wookey!'

The twins shook their heads. 'No, you've got the wrong lady,' they both said at once. 'That's not her!'

The Path to the Caves

This old lady could not possibly be Miss Wookey. Small, neat, bright-eyed and *smiling*!

She was dressed in a neatly pleated grey skirt and a pale pink twin set that fitted her beautifully. Matron had even found a string of pretty, coloured beads to put round the old lady's neck. The neat little figure also wore tights and smart black shoes. It was when she looked up at matron and asked, very meekly, 'Can I put me red 'at on now, please?' that everyone knew it *had* to be Hester.

She didn't wait for permission. The now rather grimy cherry-red hat reappeared from under the chair and was firmly squashed over the short, silky, white hair. 'Pretty, int I?' she grinned.

The police had arrived earlier that morning to take statements about the fire. It should have been a twenty-minute job, but they had not counted on meeting Miss Wookey! It took a woman police constable and a sergeant most of the morning to get anything coherent from the old lady, even with the children's help.

The children were allowed off school as they were helping the police. 'Anything to avoid a maths test!'

Maddy muttered to Dave. He only grunted in reply as he was listening very hard indeed to the woman police constable, who was trying to take down and unravel what the impossible Hester Wookey was saying.

Maddy and Dave's Mum and Dad sat at the back of the room, listening in amazement, not quite sure what to make of it all. They said nothing, but occasionally Dave could *feel* their disappointment as the story got weirder and weirder. How could their nice twins make up such a story for the *police*? But they said nothing. They may have been grown-ups, but they did have the sense to realize that they might get to the bottom of it all if they listened.

Halfway through the morning Tim arrived. He sat quietly next to Mum and Dad while the police and a social worker tied themselves in worse and worse knots as they tried to make logical sense of what had been happening. As Maddy had said, the grown-ups found the truth just too hard to cope with. At last Tim suggested that, as the police, the social worker and the twins' parents were finding Miss Wookey's story rather difficult to digest, maybe they should all go up to Wookey Hole to prove that the stone witch wasn't there any more.

This was Hester's second ride in a car. The first had been at 3.30 a.m. the previous morning, and she had been so tired and confused that she hadn't taken in much of what was happening to her. Now she saw properly the wonderful chariot that was going to transport her, without horses or anything, back to her old home. She made the woman police constable drive it very slowly, and she sat in the front seat, window wound right down, and leaning halfway out so she could see what was happening all around.

The woman police constable was not pleased: 'This is very dangerous, Miss Wookey. I could get arrested for letting you poke your head out like that!'

'Worse than that, you'll lose your hat out of the window if you lean out!' Maddy warned.

'I'm 'olding onto it!' Hester argued, clutching at the already rather bent brim.

It was quite clear that Hester had no intention of doing as she was told, so Dave and Maddy had to lean forward to pull the old lady down into her seat and keep her there firmly. After that she had to sit back, but she grumbled the whole way and arrived looking crumpled and cross, not at all the nice, sweet 'granny' who had greeted them that morning. Hester stepped out of the car, skirt tugged up, cardigan awry and her beautiful red hat squashed down over one eye.

'Let's tidy you up a little.' Maddy began to straighten the clothes. 'You're going to meet rather important people today, I expect.

'I 'ope they 'aven't made a mess of me 'ome!' Hester straightened herself up and toddled with a determined gait up to the entrance. Then, as she began to climb the walkway, she stopped and stared all around her, open-mouthed. 'What they done to it?' she asked softly. 'Where's me river and the mossy rocks, and me cress beds and the goats? Oh where's me goats?' The old lady twisted her face in sorrow as great tears ran down her cheeks and she began to cry.

'They're all gone, Miss Wookey,' Tim put in quietly. 'They died many years ago. The rocks were cleared and this path was put down so people could come and see you without tripping up on the way. Come on, everyone is waiting for us.'

But Hester Wookey didn't move. She stood rooted to the spot, looking all around her in amazement, rediscovering her little gorge for the first time in almost a thousand years. No longer was it a steep, very rocky little valley with clear water rushing and tumbling all around. Now it was something very different indeed. Now it was… tamed and encased, rather like Hester had been when the naiads had wrapped her safely in the stone which held her so still for so long.

Hester stopped in her tracks and stayed so quiet that everyone looked at her. She looked frail and shrivelled and, from the corner of each eye, more tears began to roll. Dave took her hand and squeezed it. He could imagine what she must be feeling, and it brought a lump to his throat as well.

Tim stepped forward and took Hester's other hand gently. 'Would you like a nice cup of tea Miss Wookey?'

'Tea?' She croaked, trying not to sob. 'What's tea? Oh yes, that nice sweet stuff. Do I gits it in a metal bottle or a goblet with flowers on this time?'

The twins looked at each other, quite lost. 'Thermos flask or pretty mug, I think she means,' Tim whispered.

'Come on,' he said out loud to Hester. 'It'll be in a nice flowery mug this time, I expect. But it's the same stuff and very sweet.' And with that he steered her aside to the reception at the end of one of the mill halls on their right. They went towards the entrance from where she and the children had been rescued the night before.

But Hester did not want to go in. Instead she stood still, looking all around her. Then she hung her head and started to cry again. The bright, clean images of the Mill and all its tourist attractions had smothered every last vestige of the path up to her home. 'It's all very pretty,' she sobbed. 'An' it's nice not to slip in the mud or turn me ankle on the rocks, but... but... it were me 'ome, weren't it? I were allus safe there from them that 'ated me and them murderous hounds them set on me... Now it's gorn!'

Suddenly she stopped crying and went white. 'Hounds! Where's me hound? Where's Bledig?' she demanded.

But before anyone could answer, a group of official-looking people came out from the big double doors and ushered Hester and the children inside. They were introduced as the manager, the owner's representatives and someone from the insurance company who'd come to look at the fire damage.

'And we're also very interested in the vandalism and theft that took place in the caves last night,' said a stern-looking man with a dull grey suit that exactly matched his grey moustache and grey hair. He peered very closely at the children over the top of his glasses and smiled a little. 'But I don't think you two would have been strong enough to have done that much damage.'

'What damage?' Tim appeared not to have heard the news.

The manager, a friendly faced lady with fair hair just shrugged. She looked very worried. 'You'll never believe it, but the witch has gone!'

Tim smothered a smile. 'Oh that... I've been trying to tell these officers all morning...'

But Hester would not let him finish. 'And wot about me dog, that's wot I want to know!' Hester glared around insistently. '*I'm 'ere, but where's me Bledig?*'

The manager looked at Miss Wookey in surprise. 'How did you know, Miss Wookey? The dog is gone too.'

The man from the insurance company added, 'We're possibly looking at international crime here. We suspect that it could be someone from the United States or Japan, someone with big money who fancied the witch to decorate his swimming-pool or something. It must have taken a very professional team who really understood stonecutting. Then they'd have had to have used some pretty heavy lifting gear to get the stalagmites out of the caves. The witch must have weighed a good three tonnes at least.'

'How dare he!' snorted Hester. 'I'm nothing like that big. Never 'ave bin!'

The insurance man ignored Hester's indignation and went on. 'But what intrigues us is the way it's all been done. The 'witch' and 'dog' shapes have been sort of 'peeled', leaving great chunks of calcite on the floor, and only the bits that looked most like an old lady and her hound have been removed. It's all very odd indeed. I've never known anything like it.'

The manager passed mugs of tea around, as Tim had promised. 'The reason we wanted you children and Miss Wookey to come here is partly to find out about the fire, and partly to ask if you saw anyone else around yesterday evening. Any information, however small, might give us a clue as to what happened.'

Hester did not hesitate. 'Well, youz all daft. I'm 'ere, baint I? No one nicked me. I just got fed up with sitting still all that time, and I got up an' walked off. This lad and maid 'elped a bit o' course, with tea and chicken and bread in sandy witches and special wishes an'

112

stuff. Helped a treat, but I'm 'ere! And me dog's gorn,' she added sadly. Then she lowered her brows threateningly and glared at the assembled officials. 'An' where's 'e to? I'd like to know!''

Maddy almost dropped her biscuit into the tea and Dave choked. Did Hester have to be so forthright? The robbery explanation was much easier than telling the truth, and it was what the officials wanted to believe. It was obvious no one was going to listen to what really happened. But it was too late to worry about it now. Hester was already in full flight, becoming more and more irritated as she realized she was not being believed.

At last she got up and threw her handful of biscuits across the room. 'I thought you lot were better than them lot that chased me into the caves all those years ago. You give me tea and sweet flat breads, and pretty dresses, but you think me as barmy as they did. I'm off. I'll go and get me dog and we'll go and find somewhere else to sit until someone a bit human comes along. I'll ask them naiad maids to 'elp me. I'll be right nice to them, and they'll 'elp. I knows they will. They got 'earts they 'ave! More than you lot got, and there's a fact!'

Maddy stood up and tried to calm Hester, but the old lady pushed her roughly away.

Dave ran and stood in front of the door, his short, plump arms spread wide. 'No you don't, Miss Wookey! We wished you alive, and we're going to help you now. Just give us a chance please!'

Tim put down his mug of tea and looked around at the assembled adults. He knew he was the bridge between the children and the adults, the only hope of people really believing what had happened. 'Please,' he said quietly to the officials and the police, 'please come into the caves with us and let Miss Wookey tell you her story. It does make sense if you give her a chance, really it does.'

The police sergeant stood up and pushed his notebook into his pocket. 'I'd like to go. As these three were in the caves last night, they might have seen something. Caves do funny things to your senses, I know, so however fantastic their story is it might have just enough in it to help us with the case.'

With the sergeant willing to go into the caves, the others had to follow.

To the right of the long, cool dark gallery that ran along the edge of the lake-filled chamber called 'the witch's kitchen', the stalagmite known as 'the witch' had stood for centuries. Now there was just a knob of stone on a small outcrop of rock, all that was left of the little milking stool that Hester Wookey had sat on for so long. To the left of the steps coming down into the chamber, there had once been the crouching, calcite-covered shape known as 'the dog'. That was also gone.

Hester hopped over the low parapet that separated the walkway from the little shelf that had been her whole home for nearly a thousand years. Then she settled herself on the little stool-shaped rock, holding the pose that she had held for all those ages, and she began to tell her story.

Hester's Tale

17

'I woz born in the year them cursed Normans came to our land. I woz a Saxon an' proud of it! I woz an only child, and spoiled a bit. I 'ad a pretty dress an' a fine bronze comb for me 'air. Beautiful I woz. Very beautiful. An I loved dancin'. I woz a good dancer. I loved a bit of a tune as well. I woz a merry soul.

'The priest woz a Norman, an' 'e told me to repent of me beauty and dancing an' all. 'E said I'd burn in hell for being beautiful. But 'ow can yer repent of wot yer iz? Don't make no sense nohow it don't! Anyway, all the village maids called me a witch coz I woz so pretty, like. All the swains wanted to walk with me and all the maids woz angered, as all the menfolk's heads woz turned to me. But I got proud. I didn't want to marry any of the swains who proposed like. 'Fought I woz too good for them, I did. First I turned down the miller coz 'e woz too old, then 'is son coz 'e woz too smelly, then the cowherd (well, 'e *did* have 'ooge great pock-marks!). Then there woz Gerbert the Norman servin' man, but I 'ad me eye on the lord's son 'imself! Foreign 'e may 'ave bin, but 'e woz 'ansome *and* rich. I wanted gold combs for me luvly hair, not just bronze…

'Well, as years went by, the lord's son did ask me to marry 'im, but by then I 'ad caught the eye of the bishop's nephew at Wells, so I turned 'im down flat. Broke 'is heart too,' Hester added sadly, as she looked wistfully across the icy greenness of the subterranean lake.

'But then the bishop's nephew 'eard the tales that I got me beauty by bein' a witch, and *'e* turned me down. Then the lord's son didn't want to know neither, then the cowherd and the miller and 'is son all shunned me and married the plainest matrons they could find. But that weren't hard round 'ere,' she added with a mischievous chuckle.

'By that time I was gettin' a bit old for marryin' like, so I looked after me Dad until he died, and lived on me own with me cat. I kept meself to meself, but I was good with the herbs for the cough and the dropsy, and I'd allus mix summat up for the chillun with the croup. And I'd allus go to a weddin' or a dance. I *do* love a good tune…' The old lady looked so wistful, alone on her stony perch. She kicked her feet a little as if they were remembering ancient steps she used to know.

'But folks don' like single ladies with cats. They said me herbs woz magic and stoned me cat and said 'e was me familiar. He wasn't no such thing. 'E woz me only friend. Then I started to lose me looks and get stiff all over, but the priest said beautiful folk would get punished by bein' made ugly an stiff. And that proved I woz a witch.

'By then Earl Stephen and Princess Mathilda woz 'aving their big battles over who woz goin' to be king or queen of England. There was a pox plague and the rye all got blighted. Everything woz going wrong down at the village, and they all said it woz me, and they threw me out. I woz too old to go anywhere else. So I

116

took me goats and came up here. Thought I'd be left alone up 'ere, but I wasn't. They used to come huntin' me wiv them hounds for sport on holy days.

'Didn't think it was a very holy thing to do, but you can't tell *them* that. I thought they should have forgiven me for being vain, 'cause that's wot it's all about, innit? Forgivin' and being kind and stuff.

'One day, one of them dogs they set on me slipped between some boulders in the caves and I found it whimpering with a broken leg. So I set the bone. I allus bin good at that sort of stuff. Then the dog became me friend, like. Bledig I called 'im, 'cause 'e was a bit like a wolf. 'E looked after me good, 'e did. Brought me chickens and stuff.

'But one winter the snow woz very deep, and lots o' people died, and the fever came bad. Then folk said it woz 'cause o' me, and they 'ad to get rid of me permanent like. Then that monk, Bernard or sumthing, came from Glaston to do me with 'is 'oly water. Soon as I realized wot 'is little game woz, I stayed stock-still to make 'im fink I'd turned to stone already.

'I woz too scared to move. 'E said lots of Latin stuff and waved his arms a lot. But the more I thinks about it, the more I knows that 'e weren't unkind an' angry like *our* priest. 'E offered to talk to me an' pray with me in Saxon words. I woz too scared to say anything, but I listened good. I liked 'is prayers to keep the devil away. I remembered 'em prayers good. I found them comfortin' like in the long, dark, scary hours all alone in 'ere. I used to say 'em to myself again and again.

'When Bernard woz gone I just stayed still when anyone came to poke and prod at me. Me only company was them naiad maidens. They used to sing to me, and stroke me 'air when I woz feelin' lonesome. Not that I let on I noticed, mind, I woz too proud. But I think it wuz then they wrapped me up in stone for real, for I didn't move again. Still as rock I sat with all this hard stuff makin' a shell over me. I must have looked and felt like a stone all over.

'But I still felt sad an' achy inside.

'Then when these chillun came with their 'ot tea and sandy witches, I started to feel better. I found I wasn't so stiff in the limbs as I 'ad bin. The rest 'ad done me bones some good I reckon. And for the first time in years I felt like gettin' up, and I felt like talkin' to people, and maybe even dancing a bit.

'But the stony-stuff them naiads covered me wiv was very hard. But I wriggled and wriggled until one night, I felt someone woz helpin' me off wiv it. 'Twas a bit like I could step outta me shell an' start again. Felt wunnerful it did.

'I bin cross an' moody, an' I bin bad at times, but when this lad and maid started bein' kind, and even asked God to give me a warm 'eart, well, I fought it woz all goin' to be all right. I fought I might be safe, if yer knows wot I means. I thought I didn't have to hide behind pretendin' I woz a witch any more, cause I bain't. Oh I knows a few charms against the pox and I knows a few potions to keep the agues away, but that bain't bein' a witch.

'I wants to be liked an' have grandchildren to love. I wants to come alive agin.'

At this point, Hester turned her sad stare from the lake to the men and women gathered listening to her. There were tears in her eyes. She looked so lonely. 'But if yoz don' believe me, I'll just go an' find meself somewhere else to sit,' she said softly. ''Tain't no trouble. I ain't bin loved for years, so wot's a few more?'

And with that, Hester Wookey stuck out her chin, so she resumed her old pose, and for all the world, if it hadn't been for her ridiculous red hat, anyone watching would have said the witch had never moved. In the cool, greenish half-light she looked exactly as she had always done, only a little smaller without her stone casing.

The manager and the insurance man, the owner's representative and the police sergeant and the woman police constable looked at each other in silent amazement. Behind them Mum and Dad gave little embarrassed coughs and tried to look as if they had believed the children all along.

Gently, Tim lifted a heavy, curved piece of shattered calcite from the floor, and showed how it had fitted over Hester's back during the long years she had stayed so very, very still.

The manager came and put a gentle hand on the old lady's shoulder and said, very quietly and gently, 'Miss Wookey, I fear we owe you an apology. There is no doubt you are telling the truth. Would you care to come down to the office and have another cup of tea?'

Hester's mouth hardly moved as she snapped, 'With chocolate-covered flat-breads?'

The manager looked at the twins for an explanation. 'Biscuits,' Dave explained cheerfully.

The manager nodded. 'Of course Miss Wookey. A whole packetful if you like.'

And, light as a dancer, Miss Wookey jumped down from her stool, ran past all the amazed officials and began to trot up the steps towards the cave entrance.

She turned to see everyone staring open-mouthed at her. 'Well?' she demanded. 'Wot you lot waitin' for? I bain't ever goin' to sit back there for yuz, if that's wot you thought. It gets cold in me bum!'

At first Maddy and Dave were delighted that everyone believed Hester's tale. The social worker promised she would be given a nice little place to live, warm and cosy, just like every old lady needed. Next day, they went back to school, the heroes of the class, and were in all the papers and even on television for their part in waking the Witch of Wookey Hole. Their school projects on the caves were both graded A and for the first time in weeks, everyone was pleased with them.

Despite their fears for Hester, the old lady loved the media attention, performing gleefully for anyone and everyone that asked.

A famous medieval historian came all the way from London to talk to Hester Wookey, and he confirmed that her knowledge of the time between the Norman Conquest and the accession of King Stephen was unparalleled. 'She's either telling the truth, or she's a brilliant fraud,' he said. 'And, quite confidentially, although the good lady is obviously intelligent, I don't think she is quite in the league to pull off a fraud. She's not cunning enough, if you know what I mean. She's mischievous but not devious. And she's certainly told me things I've never heard before—but they make sense and I'm convinced they are true.'

The doctors that examined her decided that she had stayed so very still for so long that her breathing and heartbeat had slowed to an absolute minimum, allowing her to stay just alive for this extraordinary length of time. 'A sort of early cryogenics', they said. And as to the near-miraculous loss of stiffness, they could only conclude that the calcium and other minerals dissolved in the Wookey water that dripped continuously down her back must have been absorbed by her bones and built them up.

But what the doctors *couldn't* answer was how she had slipped into this state to begin with. 'It's impossible,' was the conclusion of one famous specialist. 'If I didn't know better I'd say it was magic!'

Everyone laughed when he said this, knowing he must be joking. But Dave and Maddy winked at Miss Wookey as the doctor spoke.

He spotted the wink as he packed his stethoscope away. 'Who knows?' he grinned. 'The whole story is too incredible to be true. One more difficult thing to believe seems to make no odds!'

But despite everyone being happy, the owners of the caves and their managers were faced with a real problem.

The caves were pronounced safe now that everyone knew the ominous cracking and crying noises had come from poor old Hester Wookey herself. At last they could open the doors to visitors again. But there was no witch-stone to show everyone. And what was Wookey Hole without a witch?

The Sitting

18

It was Maddy who thought of it. There was no doubt in anyone's mind that it was the most brilliant idea, and the only possible solution for a most embarrassing situation.

The problem was persuading Hester to stay in place so the visitors could see her as much as possible. The place would close if there was no witch to see, and now she was so famous people were flocking from miles around to meet the *real* Witch of Wookey Hole.

The manager of the Caves had to pay Hester with two whole roast chickens, endless cups of hot tea and three packets of chocolate biscuits a day. In return Hester was supposed to sit quite still for the visitors, four days a week. No one could persuade her to do all seven. Many tourists went away disappointed because they turned up on one of Hester's days off.

Hester was even provided with a soft lamb's fleece to sit on, but the scheme did not work well. Miss Wookey was unpredictable, at best—and downright naughty at worst. The slightest whiff of a camera and she would make faces, or get out her knitting, or start telling jokes. The day the television crew arrived to film the latest episode of *Dr Who*, was the worst. She actually got up on the parapet and started to cancan because she was jealous that they weren't filming *her*!

Everyone was beside themselves with worry. Hester would not behave and, to be fair, she had sat still for so many hundreds of years, why should she?

She needed to come out of the caves and have some fun, and be able to really live for the first time in her life! But most importantly of all, she needed to feel she was wanted, not just someone to be stared at and talked about, but *really* wanted.

During half-term Dave and Maddy took turns at sitting with the old lady and chatting to her while she was supposedly sitting still. But they soon had enough of this too. The weather had cheered up at last and they wanted to be out on their bikes and seeing their friends. Mum and Dad weren't sure it was good for them to be stuck in the caves all day either.

One evening Dave was sprawled on the sitting-room floor, playing his computer games. 'I think those carved figures that came to life and led us in the chase across the hills would make a terrific platform game, don't you?'

'How do you mean?' Maddy was only half-listening. She was reading her magazine, and was always bored when her brother started talking about computer games.

'I mean, if someone invented a game where fairground figures came alive, especially ones like Neptune and the naiads, it could be brill. There could be some evil dude like the wishing wizard casting spells and the good guys coming to life and protecting the children at the fair. It could be a real action game. There could be spells being thrown around like basketballs, and the figures making the gallopers come alive and giving people rides out of danger with all sorts of cheats through to different levels… diving into wobbly mirrors and coming out through the ghost train ride and stuff! A bit like we did, but more so!'

Suddenly Maddy sat up straight and thumped the coffee table so hard that the cat leaped across the room in terror.

'That's it!'

'What is?

'Carved figures, you dope! Don't you see? You don't, do you? You're so thick at times.'

Dave scratched his head and resumed the endless chase of fearsome creatures from the deep across his TV screen. 'Weird,' he muttered.

But Maddy was not going to be brushed aside. She jumped up and stood in front of the screen.

'Oi, wotchit!' Dave moaned. 'I'm about to destroy my fifteenth Giant of Doom!' and he threw his slipper at her.

'But don't you *see*?' Maddy persisted, throwing the slipper back, 'that if someone *carved* a portrait of the witch, I mean Miss Wookey, and put it in her place, then everyone's problems would be solved! The caves would have their witch back, and Miss Wookey would be able to retire and have fun like she needs to. Bribing her to sit still all day is all very well, but it's not really fair on her and she is… well, *naughty*, isn't she? All this dancing around on the parapet is so dangerous, but she just can't help herself—and she's going to fall into that lake one day, I'm sure!'

Dave put his control pad down and picked up a pencil. He started sketching how a statue of Hester Wookey would look. After a few moments, he grinned.

'You know, I hate to admit it, but you're right! Bags I get to ring Tim!' and he jumped up to get to the phone.

But Maddy met him with a flying tackle at the knees. 'My idea!' she laughed as she rolled over and grabbed the receiver. '*I* get to tell!'

The sculptor was quite a famous one from London. He liked doing unusual things, and had become well known when he had left a huge fibreglass crocodile in the middle of Oxford Circus one morning, and the traffic could not get past. He thought the idea of sculpting Miss Wookey was great fun, and accepted the commission on condition he could do a second piece depicting Miss Wookey dancing on the parapet dressed as a cancan girl, to put in the museum.

Hester was frightened and tickled all at once by the idea of being sculpted. But she insisted that the twins came with her to London. She wouldn't let matron or anyone else go either. It had to be Maddy and Dave or she wasn't going. So the trip to meet the sculptor was arranged for a Saturday. Mum (very unreasonably, Maddy thought) refused to let the twins have any more time off school now the fuss had died down.

'You will have to sit still for the sculptor, Miss Wookey,' the children warned her as they boarded the train. Miss Wookey was not listening. She had wound the window down and was leaning out as far as she could. 'You two sure this bain't a real dragon?' she asked suspiciously.

'It most definitely *is* a real dragon—and it won't let us get out again if you don't come here and sit still.' Maddy announced firmly.

Dave bribed her with sherbet lemons, and Maddy

pushed her quite firmly until the old lady was coaxed back to her seat. For the hour and a half they were travelling, Hester Wookey did not stop asking questions, not only of Maddy and Dave, but every other passenger as well. Up and down she went, asking people what they had in their sandy witches, poking her bony finger between the bread slices to see for herself. Then she walked between the seats wanting to try on any hats she saw, snatching them from people's heads without a by-your-leave for anyone.

Thankfully, most people took the old lady's antics in good part, although one old man called her a witch and threatened to call the guard. Hester bristled visibly and struck a very witch-like pose, fingers splayed, eyes glowering, and began to mutter what the children now knew was Middle English for 'baa baa black sheep,' but the poor man did not know. He grabbed his hat and briefcase and got out at the next stop, promising to write to the railway company and complain.

The children sighed with relief when they pulled into Paddington Station. But they then had the problem of manoeuvring Hester through the crowds, and getting her to walk instead of standing gawping up at the station's magnificent iron spans that held the great glass roof in wide sweeps above them.

At last, a tall, corpulent middle-aged man with a thick black beard started running towards them, waving frantically. He was dressed in jeans that were patched in purple at the knees and a multicoloured velvet coat, made out of what looked like huge squares of red-and-green upholstery fabric.

As he approached he swept off the small embroidered black velvet cap he wore and swept an elaborate bow. 'Miss Wookey—it must be Miss Wookey with a bone structure like yours. You are, if I may say so, the *epitome* of Saxon beauty. I am delighted to meet you.' And he took her hand and kissed it.

Hester stood stock-still, opened her mouth, but was speechless! Then very slowly she went red, from her neck, up to her cheeks, her ears and even the tip of her nose blushed.

The children gawped, exchanged glances and looked at the sculptor, who was gazing at Hester with genuine admiration. This was no flannel. He really did find her beautiful! And to call her a 'Saxon beauty' must have been the greatest compliment she had ever been paid.

Then the sculptor turned to each of the twins, and shook their hands more conventionally. 'I'm Nick Harris,' he said, smiling. 'Do you mind going by bus?'

The twins and Hester Wookey were all too amazed to speak. Even on the bus journey, which Maddy was dreading, Hester behaved herself almost immaculately as she stared open-mouthed and in wide-eyed adoration at this gentleman who had obviously completely won her heart!

Nick lived in a narrow Edwardian house, with a wooden studio built behind the kitchen. The place smelled of clay and a strange metallic tang of chicken wire. The windows opened onto a tangled garden strewn with late, multicoloured tulips, American currant bushes and the fallen, untidy blossom from two twisted old pear trees.

The children were given cans of fizz and left to their own devices with a pair of overfed tabby cats, who were sunning themselves upside down in the long grass, but

Miss Wookey was taken inside the studio, sat on a tall stool, and photographed from every angle. She was so amazed by Nick's fascination with her bone structure that, despite the frightening flashes, she sat as still for him as she had for the last few hundred years. 'Sad I bain't got me pretty pink dress on though!' she sighed. 'I'd have liked a picture o' myself like that!'

Nick took four whole rolls of black and white film before producing French bread and cheese for lunch. They sat at a white metal table in the garden examining their hands and each other's faces in the different angles of light, as Nick explained about bone structure, and how everyone had a beauty, but some hid it under anger or make-up, and that others were just too frightened to let it show. Nick drew with thick charcoal on rough paper, to show how even the twins with their round faces and podgy hands would develop into fascinating shapes as they grew older.

'Come into my photographic studio and help me develop the films, and you'll see what I mean,' he suggested.

'Do you mind if we go inside, Miss Wookey?' Dave asked.

The old lady flapped her fingers to signal the children to go away. 'I'm fine my lovlies. I bain't sat in the sunshine for many a long year. It'll do me bones good, I'm sure. Run along.'

As they peered in the red gloom of the sculptor's bathroom-cum-darkroom, the children saw, with fascinated amazement, picture after picture of a beautiful old lady appearing on the wet paper, gleaming and delicate, as the images were hung to dry on a little washing line above the bath.

When the blackouts were taken down, the twins gasped at the superb shape of the fine-lined face, taut skin on strong bones, with white hair combed back to show a wide, intelligent forehead above dark, determined blue eyes.

'Eyes put in with smutty fingers,' Dave said suddenly.

'What's that?' Nick asked.

'Oh it's just a west country saying. If you have Celtic blood in you, you tend to have blue eyes, but dark all around them, so people say your eyes were put in with smutty fingers. She must have Celtic blood, as well as Saxon.'

'Hardly surprising!' Nick smiled as he held a rapidly drying print up to the natural light from the window. 'Now here you are. Black-and-white photography shows bone structure better than colour, but she really is incredibly beautiful once you stop to look.'

'She's quite nice inside too, once she stops being frightened and suspicious,' Dave said kindly. 'In fact, she's rather fun. She does and says all the things I wouldn't dare to, but wish I could!'

Maddy tried to look disapproving, but knew what he meant. She peered out of the window to try and see Miss Wookey in the garden below. 'Do you think we ought to go and see if she's all right? We've been up here for ages. She might be doing something pretty dreadful down there without anyone to keep an eye on her.'

Nick with his added height could see further into the garden. 'She's well away. I made her work hard this morning,' Nick smiled.

And, to be sure, when the twins stood on tiptoe they could see the old lady was sound asleep and snoring loudly.

Window-boxes

19

Nick blew copies of some of the best photos up to a very large size, and sent them to Hester. She had them framed, and then packed them away carefully. She was very excited; she was moving out of the nursing home, where she had been staying, into her own little warden flat.

Hester was ten times as old as most of the old dears in the home, but she was ten times as lively. 'It's just as if she's stored up all her energy over the years, and it's all coming out at once,' matron said nervously. 'I do hope she doesn't shock too many of the residents in the other flats. Some of them are a little old-fashioned.'

Maddy and Dave felt they could make no promises on that score, and left as soon as they politely could.

There was a party for Hester the day she left the home. Everyone gave her something to make her new flat comfy. It was a Saturday so the twins could help too. Maddy had brought a hammer and nails to hang the framed photographs in the new sitting-room, and Tim arrived with the furniture to help put everything in place.

'I woz born at this time o' year,' Hester said wistfully, staring out over the communal gardens. 'My mam's little spring flower I woz. I'll go an' pick some o' them flowers for me room. They'll look very pretty in a pot o' water.'

'I don't think people would like you picking *those*,' Maddy warned gently. 'They are there to make the gardens look nice. Dave is good at gardening; perhaps he'll help you fill a window-box.'

'Wot's one o' them when it's at 'ome?' Hester demanded.

'It's a big box you can put up here by the window and fill with flowers. It's your own little garden,' Tim explained.

'I'd like one o' them!' Hester chuckled. But when Maddy and Dave came to visit Hester the next day after school, they were met by a very worried-looking warden. 'I don't know *what* she's up to, I'm sure,' the poor lady wrung her hands in desperation, 'but for some reason there's lots of muddy water coming from her floor through to the ceiling below. She won't let me into her flat and Miss Barnes who lives downstairs has had cold water dripping down since yesterday, and everything in her flat has got all damp and stained.

Dave and Maddy looked at each other. Their hearts sank. That was what Gran's flat had been like. What *was* Miss Wookey up to this time?

'I must say,' the warden added timidly, 'she is the most dauntingly determined lady I have ever met. She won't let me even go and see her. She won't let me in at all!'

'We know!' Maddy said. 'Come on Dave, you go first—you're less likely to get cross with her than me.'

Dave knocked, and Hester opened her door gingerly. 'Oh, it's you. *You* can come in. Is the maiden there as well?' Half afraid of what he might see, Dave put his head around the door. And he was right to be worried, for arranged in a row under the window, were three large, sagging cardboard boxes, filled with soil, and stuffed with flowering plants.

'In't they grand?' the old lady beamed, flinging the door open wide. 'I only wish I knowed where me poor ol' Bledig woz. 'E loved flowers too. 'E used to smell 'em good, then 'e give 'em a good waterin'!' And the old lady beamed and chuckled with happy memories.

'Oh, Miss Wookey, where did you get those?' Maddy asked in suspicious horror.

'Out the garden, course! But I bain't picked 'em! You told me not to pick 'em. I digged 'em up with me fingers. I'll look after them good, I will. Look, I gives 'em a good waterin' twice a day,' and she picked up a jug from the table, and proceeded to pour the contents all over the plants.

From below came a sharp thump thump, as the poor lady underneath got yet another drenching—the water seeped from the sodden boxes, through the carpet, and deluged the ceiling below.

'Oh Miss Wookey!' Dave said. 'You've made window-boxes! Aren't they...' he swallowed as he thought quickly... '*pretty*!'

Hester crossed her skinny arms and leaned against the table grinning.

Dave did not want to shatter Hester's happiness, but it had to be done. 'But that isn't the way to make them. I think we'd better take you to the garden centre and get you properly set up.'

Hester's face clouded. 'Youz sayin' me boxes bain't pretty enough?' she looked hurt.

'It's not that they aren't pretty enough, they aren't *strong* enough,' Maddy explained. 'Look, the water's going everywhere.'

Then Dave had an inspired thought: he knew how he could make Hester understand. 'The water drips through the ceiling here like it used to drip through the caves, and the lady downstairs doesn't like it. It trickles into her hair and down her back . She feels like you did in the cave. She's all cold and wet and miserable.'

Hester lost her smile and looked very remorseful. 'Oo, I didn't know that. I bet she don't like it. I used to hate the cold dripping down me neck. I'll take her a present,' and, before anyone could stop her, Hester had picked three of the best tulips from the soggy 'window-boxes' and had darted out of the door and run downstairs with them.

'Oh well,' said the warden when she saw the mess, 'with the money she's getting from the newspapers for her life story, we can soon clear this lot up. I think a visit to the garden centre would be a good idea. We'll get the handyman to fix proper brackets for the boxes outside her window, then hopefully all will be well.'

Dave shook his head. 'Not with Miss Wookey, I'm afraid.'

By the end of the day, Hester was all set up with a very fine window-box full of pansies and lobelias. The box even had a little bird table screwed to one end.

Hester positively glowed with happiness. It was one of those moments when everyone could see that the sculptor had been right. In her own way, Hester was very beautiful. And she wasn't an evil witch, or even a nasty person. She was just someone who had been hurt and frightened all her life, and needed a little love.

'Oh my,' she sighed. 'I *do* wish Bledig was here!'

'Who is Bledig?' The warden asked. 'She keeps talking about him—or her.'

Maddy paled. 'That's a good point actually. Bledig is her dog. He came to life at the same time as she did, but he didn't come out of the caves with her. Mind you, I'm not sorry. He wasn't the sort of cute little doggy I'd like to take for a walk.'

'The guides called him a "rock-weiler",' Dave chimed in. 'And I don't think they were far wrong. He's mean! Not at all the little cute Dougally-dog that his stone used to look like.'

Suddenly, the twins looked at each other in horror. 'And he's still loose in the caves!' they squealed. 'He might go for someone. Help!'

'Come on Miss Wookey!' Maddy tugged at the old lady's hands. 'We've got to find him, before he does something dreadful!'

Hester glanced regretfully at her pretty window-box. 'Yes, I'll come. I do miss um. 'E might be pinin' for me!'

At the caves, the manager looked relieved. 'There have been reported sightings of a stray dog, Miss Wookey. And people have heard strange scratchings and howlings coming from all around. I've heard it myself in fact, and it's very spooky. But we didn't realize it was *your* dog. We just thought all our troubles were starting again.'

'Cummon then,' Hester was already at the office door. 'Wot yuz waitin' for then?'

The twins had always thought the path down to the

caves was exciting and adventurous, but today it seemed drear and dismal. Perhaps it was the contrast with Hester's bright new flat and the sunny day outside. But this was what Hester Wookey must have felt for so many, many years, all on her own down here. It must have been what Gran had felt like in her gloomy London flat. The twins shivered. No wonder Hester did not like being 'on duty' four days a week in the caves. The sooner the sculpture was finished the better.

Their footsteps echoed and they trod the stone and concrete pathways down, down, down to what had always been called the 'witch's kitchen'. Here was the lone stone stool where Hester had sat for so long, all alone except for her faithful dog, who had crouched, also covered with calcite, behind her, waiting for someone who cared enough to wish them both alive. Now there were just empty places and fragments of broken rock where the prisoners had broken free.

Hester sat on her parapet and started to cry.

'Bledig!' she wept. 'How could I forget you? I wuz sittin' in me nice, warm, comfy place, and yuz were down here in the cold and wet, without even a bit o' chicken to warm yer belly. Oh Bledig, 'ow could I? I is just a wicked old woman, I is!' Then she started to call and whistle for her dog, but there was no answer. Frantically the old lady jumped up again and started to run here and there, peering into all sorts of nooks and crannies and clambering over rock falls that even the guides had not explored before.

But after an hour and a half, there was neither sight nor sound of the dog.

The manager looked at her watch. 'It's well after closing time, Miss Wookey. I don't know about you, but

I'm hungry and tired. After I've had my dinner I'll pop out to the late supermarket and get some dog food and I'll come back and leave it out near where Bledig used to be. We'll ask the guides to keep an eye out for him too.'

Hester could do nothing but agree. 'Will yuz call me if yuz hears anything?'

'Of course we will. Immediately!' the manager assured her kindly. Together the four of them walked sadly out of the caves, and locked the big wooden gates behind them.

'I don't like to think of 'im all alone down there. 'E's a good dog is Bledig. But 'e do get cross when 'e's 'ungry 'e do.'

Indeed, he must have been very hungry, for in the morning the dog food the manager had put down was all gone.

Under the 20 the Mendips

The manager kept her promise to put food out for Bledig every day. The howlings and scrapings continued for a few days, but then they suddenly stopped and the dog food was no longer eaten in the mornings. Hester wandered around calling and calling, but apart from the occasional faint bark and whimper, which could have come from anywhere, there was no sign of Bledig.

Hester point-blank refused to sit in her place until she knew what had happened to her beloved dog. Meanwhile she got more and more daring as she clambered here and there looking for her friend. Terrified for the old woman's safety, the manager called in two professional army cavers to accompany the old lady. Her insistence on going deeper and deeper into hitherto undiscovered regions became alarming. Everyone except Hester was terrified. She allowed herself to be dressed in a boiler suit and she rammed a caver's helmet over her red hat (which she would *not* take off), but she sniffed at the ropes the cavers tried to tie round her waist. 'I weren't' born to be 'ung!' she snapped. 'I bain't never 'aving no rope around me waist. It might slip to me neck, then I'll be done for!'

There was no arguing with Hester, and she knew each twist and turn so intimately that the cavers could not catch her to rope her up anyway. Indeed, she was so small and lithe, she seemed to be able to wriggle in and out of very narrow crevices, spaces that made the men's eyes water at the thought of them.

On the fourth day of looking for Bledig, no one had heard even the slightest whimper. Hester was even more frantic than ever. She forgot all about her window-box and her new home, all she could think about was Bledig. She was standing at the gates an hour before the caves opened, dressed in her gear, and ready to go.

The twins had a day off school because of teacher training and Mum and Dad allowed them to go along to help, but neither of them were relishing the trip. The cave manager turned up jangling her keys and looking doubtful. 'Look Miss Wookey, I've had a word with the local vet, and he's convinced your dog can't possibly be alive. It's four weeks since you were found, and in all that time he's not eaten properly. It's sad but he must have fallen somewhere and got trapped. He must be dead. Why don't we just call it a day? A friend of mine's poodle has just had puppies, I'd gladly take you to see them, and perhaps you could choose one?'

'Wot, 'an let me best friend down? 'E protected me when I wuz bein' witchyfied. 'E chose to stay with me. I bain't gonna desert 'im now. Corse 'e bain't dead. 'E bain't eaten for several 'undred years, wot's another few weeks to 'im? But I knows wot I knows and 'e be hurt somewhere. 'E needs me, and I'm going on until I find 'im.'

Hester said nothing, but with a grim set to her determined jaw, the old lady glared at the manager until she opened the doors.

The poor woman had not been trained to deal with people like Hester. She was a very determined lady. It was no wonder people had called her a witch once. The manager looked at the worried Hester, then at her own neat watch. 'Well, the cavers won't be here for another half-hour at least, so promise me you'll just wait somewhere sensible until they come?'

'I promise!' Hester drooped her head and muttered as she kicked at a bit of loose rock.

Maddy and Dave knew instinctively that Hester was lying, but all they could do was stick with her and try to keep her out of trouble for as long as possible. But they could tell it was not going to be easy.

At first, Hester behaved reasonably. She scurried down to her old place by the lake, and called and called. But the twins could tell she was getting pan-icky. 'I knows in me bones somethin' is wrong!' she said, and started to fidgit, then to walk around and around, peering this way and that and mumbling to herself.

'No wonder people thought she was a witch,' Dave whispered, 'hark at her yattering away!'

Suddenly the old lady stopped and glared at the children under her dark eyebrows. 'Know wot I 'ates?'

'What's that?' Dave asked.

'I 'ates the fact that Neptune and 'is fancy girls run with their blessed river through every nook and cranny of this 'ere place. They must know exactly where that dog o' mine is, and they're not tellin' me. That's wot!'

139

'Well, have you tried asking them?' Maddy ventured.

'Oh they'll never listen to me!' Hester moaned, her face closed and tight, looking every bit as ugly and cross as when the twins first met her. 'Wot's the point?' And with that she slipped behind a stalagmite and disappeared completely.

The twins dashed to the spot and although they felt this way and that, they could not detect any place where the cantankerous old woman could have gone. At last Dave looked up and saw a small crevice above their heads. 'She couldn't have gone up *there* could she?' He looked horrified.

Maddy shook her head in disbelief. She stretched up her hands and found there was a good knob above her head that she could pull on, and there was a step-like protrusion by her left knee, that she could stand on...

Within seconds she, too, was up and also out of sight.

'Maddy? Maddy!' Dave wailed. He was no scaredy-cat, but being alone in the half-lit caves on this strange day when everything seemed different was beginning to get to him.

He stood staring up at the narrow dark space above his head and felt his chest go tight and his back go cold. '*Maddy!*' he screamed.

Suddenly her round face appeared right above his own. She was grinning. She put out a hand and offered to help him up. 'Come on,' she urged. 'It's easy.'

Dave hesitated. 'Shouldn't we wait here? The army cavers will be here soon and we'll need to meet them.'

'But if we don't follow Miss Wookey, they'll never find any of us. It's like a Swiss cheese up here, and she's already out of sight. I know which way she's gone though. If we follow now we'll be OK. If we wait it'll be disastrous!'

Dave still hesitated. 'But it's too dangerous. We need the professionals. If we all slip, none of us will ever be found.'

'What are the chances of us all slipping, though?' Maddy persisted. 'Surely if one of us falls, the other can go back for help. It's much safer this way, trust me.'

Dave didn't entirely trust his sister. But he couldn't out-argue her either. So he heaved himself up as she directed and switched his caving lamp on. But after one flicker, nothing happened. 'I can't go on,' he said with relief. 'My lamp doesn't work.'

'Mine does,' Maddy's voice came from behind a faint glow somewhere in the blackness ahead. 'I'll warn you of any problems. Just follow me and stick close.'

Dave undid his beloved Liverpool scarf and trailed it behind him so it hung out of the passage entrance. Although it was dangling behind the stalagmite, if anyone was really looking they were bound to see it... he hoped.

The crack wound steadily onwards, going uphill at first, then turning several sharp bends and plunging quite steeply down. The rock was dry, and the children found they could grip the sides quite firmly and control their slide. 'We'll be able to get out of this OK,' Maddy assured him. 'It'll be easy to climb up again.'

But hardly had she spoken when her foot slipped and she felt herself plummeting down, down, sliding, spinning out of control. It felt like she was falling down a huge sheet of flat rock that had been turned to lie at a forty-five degree angle in the middle of what must have been an enormous cavern. She did not scream;

she just gasped, closed her eyes and prayed she wouldn't die as she flapped around uselessly for something to catch hold of.

Dave could not see what was happening. The faint, intermittent flicker from his helmet lamp showed him nothing, except a steep drop ahead. Maddy's lamp just flashed and bounced, then seemed to go out—or else she had fallen somewhere even deeper, out of sight.

He could hear a lot of bumping noises. Then there was silence.

Dave slithered backwards a short way, trying to find firm, sure rocks to lean against. But there was nothing except the slope he was sitting on. It felt as if he was floating alone in space. He told himself not to panic; he could not be far from the tunnel.

He held his breath, trying to listen for the slightest sound that might tell him that his sister was alive, and where she was. There was nothing except the muddy, gravely sound of his own shoes as he eased his position in the rocks. Everything was black. It was a blackness of such heavy intensity, he could not ever have imagined it before. On top of him were thousands of tons of Mendip hillside. Ahead lay unknown danger of who knew what size? Behind him was a difficult and treacherous climb out with no light, and who knew what pitfalls on the way? He breathed deeply and once again fought the rising panic that felt as if it was going to consume him.

'Mads?' he called tentatively.

No reply. Nothing. The sound fell dead against the rock.

'Maddy?' He shouted this time, but his voice sounded hollow and alone.

Still nothing.

'Maddy?' He was screaming now. '*MADDY!*' He was trying not to cry. There was no answer, only a soulful echo. He was trying to think clearly, but the darkness seemed to press in on him, blotting out his thoughts and filling him with cold, lonely fear…

Alone in the Dark

21

The cavers had arrived to find the main chambers empty. It was still too early for the public to start arriving. The manager had warned the men that Miss Wookey was being difficult, and that she might have run off somewhere, but that the children would be waiting.

But there was no one down there. The caves were empty.

The leader, a tall man with hands like vices and a voice in his boots, had found the Liverpool scarf. It was no longer dangling in a telling fashion as Dave had hoped. It had slipped into a puddle at the foot of the stalagmite that hid the small crevice that Hester and the twins had crawled into. The men did not look up. They simply walked around, searching everywhere obvious. After twenty minutes or so, they gave up and went back to the office.

'They must have gone home,' the leader said. 'There's no sign of them. Call us when they want to go looking again.'

The secretary nodded pleasantly. 'I'll tell the manager when she's off the phone,' she promised.

The men were about to get into their car when a frantic figure came running and waving towards them.

'They haven't left the caves,' she gasped as she caught up with them. 'I'd know. Miss Wookey would have come for her tea and biscuits. She'd have wanted to tell me whether she'd found the dog or not... She hasn't come—and neither have the children, I just *know* they're in there!'

The two cavers did not waste a second. One pulled huge skeins of climbing rope and a first aid box from the boot of the car, while another tapped out the number of the local cave rescue service. Then they swung into action.

Time ticked slowly by. The rescue service and the army cavers spread out through the chambers, but found nothing. A specially trained dog had arrived by mid morning, and the caves were closed to visitors.

'I do hope that Miss Wookey is safe and has found her Bledig,' the manager moaned into a mug of very strong coffee. 'I can't bear going through all this again.'

Meanwhile, Dave was sitting rigid with terror at the top of the slope where Maddy, and presumably Hester as well, had slid into the all-consuming blackness below.

He had not moved a single muscle for... how long? One hour, two? Maybe it had been all day, or maybe just a few minutes. He had no way of telling. Time simply did not exist in this blackness. He tried counting his heartbeats as the blood pounded through his ears. At last he could understand how Hester had stayed so still and unmoving for centuries.

Fear had that effect.

How he wished he had not followed Maddy. He should have done what he knew to be right—to stay put and wait for the professionals. It was always foolish to go into a cave of any sort without a properly led party. He knew that… but in retrospect what could he have done? Said no?

He wished he had done just that.

Suddenly he felt his right leg start twitching as cramp and tremors set in. Gingerly he eased it a little straighter. To his surprise, he did not slip. He found, in fact, he had eased himself a little higher. He breathed deeply. He wished the wishing wizard were here, so he could wish himself out of this place and get help for the others.

But the naiads had said that the wishing wizard was only an automaton, and that wishes were granted by people who loved life. Easy for them to say…

Yet in the distance there was a faint sound of trickling water. The naiads had said they flowed through all the caves in the water… perhaps if he called loudly enough, they might hear him and tell someone…

He called out tentatively once or twice, but his voice sounded so silly in the lonely dark. How could anyone hear him? Even the wonderful, magical naiads could not hear him here. Suddenly he had a horrid thought. If the river people were in their watery form, did they have ears? Could they hear him? But they might only be able to speak and move in their carved forms. When they were water they could probably do nothing!

In desperation he called again, but louder and more urgently this time. Then he jumped, making himself slip alarmingly, for a soft sound came back to him out of the blackness.

'This… place is… too dry… dry… dry… we cannot… help… help… help…!' the faint voice echoed and whispered from everywhere all at once.

He looked around in the total blackness. For a few seconds the memory of the voice made him feel less alone. Then he felt worse, knowing someone was there but who could not help. It was all up to him now. And all he could think of was the time they were all on top of the Mendips and Neptune was giving Miss Wookey a good talking to. To give Miss Wookey a warm heart they had used something stronger than a common or garden wish… Now he would have to find another special sort of wish. He would have to love his annoying sister and the irritable old Miss Wookey enough to actually *do* something himself.

He would have to believe in Life, as the naiad had said, or they would all die here.

'Please God, help me get this right!' he said quietly into the dark. For now he knew exactly what he needed to do.

He would turn the whole thing into a computer game! First he tried to picture the way they had come in his head. Then he pretended he was Taffo the purple Mouse scurrying along various passages trying to find the cheese before the evil cat got him. He found himself breathing more normally. Things didn't feel so bad now. In the absolute dark it was easy to imagine the levels and passages very clearly. He found he could even 'see' the way the tunnels had run in his head… up, up, along, down, steady and dry, easy to get up again, as Maddy had said. So now all he had to do was to go back along it all in reverse…

Up, and behind him… He reached above his head and groped for handholds. His heart missed a beat as he realized he was already out of whatever tunnel he had been in. It was open space all around. His fingers met nothing except the slab he was sitting on. He would just have to wriggle backwards on his bottom and try and find the entrance. But what would happen if he found a *different* entrance to another tunnel going nowhere? He turned his face this way and that, hoping to feel a tell-tale breeze against his cheek.

The great Nothing. That was what would happen. He had to get it right. 'Think computer game; think Taffo the Mouse,' he told himself. He didn't need to close his eyes to visualize. He just needed to keep the bright images of the purple mouse in front of his eyes. It was a lot less frightening than the dark. The dark was the problem. He wouldn't be nearly so scared if his lamp worked. He wouldn't be so terrified of going wrong. Going back and having another shot would not be so daunting…

He thumped at his helmet lamp and twiddled the switch. If only he could get a glimpse around for a few seconds it might give him a vital clue as to which way to push himself…

Suddenly the lamp did flash on, but then he wished it hadn't…

He was indeed sitting at the lip of a huge cavern, bigger than any he had seen so far. He was perched on the top of a steeply sloping slab, which tipped endlessly into the dark. His lamp went out again before he had managed to look up at the way out. He froze again. If only he had not known how perilous his position was. If only he had not looked. He knew he must not let the dark *Nothingness* overtake him again. He had to believe the others were still alive. He had to believe in life. He had to make this wish that they were all safely out of here come true!

Gingerly he eased his backside up the slab, glad that his trainers were gripping well on the rock below. Within four or five gentle shoves, he felt rock against his back. 'Taffo the Mouse! Visualize!' he told himself out loud. He needed action replays! How had he come down, from the right or the left? He spread his arms behind him, feeling around on both sides.

But he could only find loose stones. Some slid from under his fingers as he touched them. He held his breath as he heard the small clattering sounds bouncing past him and down, down... he pushed his fingers into his ears. He did not want to know how far down they fell.

Dave swallowed hard and shuffled a little to the left, but his way was blocked by what felt like a large rock fall. He hoped it had happened thousands of years ago... what if there would be another one today? No one knew what sort of precarious boulders were hanging over his head...

He mustn't think about it.

He couldn't have come from that side anyway. It didn't 'feel' right, so he slid himself back the other way. Slowly, grittily, he shifted himself, centimetre by centimetre, groping and feeling with his fingers until he felt...

Cloth?

Terrified of what he might feel next, he pulled his hand back. The last thing he wanted to find here was a skeleton!

But he moved so quickly that he jerked his whole body and found himself slipping down the slab. In panic he tried to claw with his fingernails at the smooth rock face as he pushed with the toes of his trainers against the muddy, inevitable slide.

22
Bledig

The hand that caught Dave's wrist was indeed bony, but it was no skeleton. The skin was cool, but alive. And with amazing strength, the fingers held Dave firmly as he checked his slide.

'Take it easy!' the voice croaked. 'Don't panic or yuz a gonna. 'Ere, put yer 'and up to the right of yuz, and there be a piece o' rock like a jug, got it? Right, now pull yersel' up.'

'Miss Wookey!' Dave breathed in relief and amazement, I thought you woz—I mean I thought you *were* dead!'

The voice chuckled. 'No, I bain't dead yet. But I think I fell asleep or summat. I gits all sort of stupid and stiff down in these 'ere caves. 'S funny, I could 'ear yuz callin', but I couldn't do nothing about it. Couldn't move, like before. I really 'ad to make myself move when I 'eard yuz slippin' an' all. I knew yuz needed me, and I 'ad to do summat. After all, yuz an the maid 'elped me afore now.'

'Didn't you see Maddy come past here? She fell down that great slab before I came through.'

'Woz that th' maid? I did see a fallin' light and wot might have been hands flailing about, but I woz too far gone to be able to move. I woz like I woz before, all

150

gorn still. We ought to get out of 'ere afore I goes off again. Then we can get one of them girt big men to come an' look for 'er. Even I don't think I can get down that bit and back.'

'Do hurry Miss Wookey…' Dave urged. 'I can't hear her, and I'm so frightened for her.'

'I knows 'ow yuz a-feelin'. I still can't find Bledig neither. Though this used to be 'is favourite spot. Cummon, this way.'

And following Hester's scratching, scraping sounds, Dave soon found he was back in the passage which was indeed very close by and not at all long. Then suddenly, in a way that was almost tangible, there was light ahead.

Dave rushed at it so fast that he knocked Hester aside, as he squeezed past her and almost fell out of the opening.

The relief on the faces of the cave rescue team below was a joy to see. They had just been equipping themselves with aqualungs to search the lake below the witch's stool.

The team helped Dave down, and then Hester.

'Where's the girl? Is she with you?' asked the man with the deep voice.

Dave started to burble everything out at once, but a slim young woman in a wet suit made him slow down so everyone could understand what was being said.

It took the rescue party less than half an hour to find Maddy and bring her out. She had broken a leg and had knocked herself unconscious, but apart from that there was no great damage done.

She came round as she was being carried out on a stretcher. 'I'm never, ever, coming to this place again,' she moaned.

'That's a shame,' Dave said, 'I've just been told that next Monday Nick the sculptor will be delivering his statue of Miss Wookey, and the unveiling will be on Saturday. We've been invited as guests of honour, front row seats and all!'

Maddy's head and leg hurt too much for her to care, although she knew she would not miss an event like that, even if she'd broken every bone in her body!

Hester Wookey turned up for the unveiling in a brand new suit. Red, of course, with a big floppy red hat to go with it. But she wasn't herself. She hadn't been since the cave rescue. She looked very, very sad. 'I knows Bledig's not dead,' she kept moaning, 'I just knows it! But where is 'e?'

She managed to put on a smile as she entered the caves. After all, this was the sort of day she *loved*. Everyone was there to make a fuss of her. Several photographers were there, together with film crews from local and national television. After the unveiling she had to do a special interview with the paper that had bought her story. She had all the ingredients to thoroughly enjoy herself—except that Bledig was still missing.

The sound of music was coming from outside. Hester stopped feeling sorry for herself and turned to smile at the procession of children coming through the gates. With commendable dignity, she avoided dancing as she led the parade of scouts and guides down the steps, through her old home. In the chamber where she had sat for so long, everything was floodlit for television lights. The chamber was hung with brightly glittering bunting made out of silver and gold foil that swayed and gleamed in the stirring air. The water of the great green lake had several rafts floating on it, each filled with several rows of seats.

Tim, the cave guide who had helped them so much, was showing people to their places on the rafts. He looked as if he was more worried by the erratic wobbling than anyone else.

Gingerly, the mayor and lady mayoress were treading across the swaying connections between the floating platforms, until they sat down with obvious relief on the central one, right in front of the sculpture when it was unveiled. Next to them sat Nick, the artist, dressed in a grey suit. He looked so proper that the children didn't recognize him until he grinned and waved at them. He was still wearing his little black embroidered hat. Dave ran across the rafts to greet him. Maddy had to stay on the main walkway in a wheelchair that had been specially brought down for her.

A strong male nurse from the hospital had helped Tim to carry her down the steps to get to the ceremony. Maddy's leg hurt a lot, but she knew she would not have missed this day for the world. She would not get the best view from the front, but she would have the privilege of sitting next to the sculpture when the purple velvet cloth was pulled aside, so she knew she would be in the photographs and the television footage.

Hester behaved herself beautifully. She did not dance, or dive into side-chambers, or say anything rude about anyone. Instead, she sat on her chair next to Nick, holding his hand nervously while the musicians from the local silver band had collected on the steps, filling the chamber with swelling sounds.

At first they played waltzes and marches, but as the

seats were taken, the music slowed to some lively early medieval ballads that Hester obviously recognized, for she put her head on one side and smiled a little wistfully. 'My Bledig would have liked this,' she sighed. ''E'd 'ave liked it a lot. That was 'is favourite tune!'

At last there was silence. The Mayor stood up, a little uncertainly, on the rocking raft. Then, rustling his sheaf of papers, he coughed, and started to make what everyone feared was going to be a long speech. But scarcely had he started, when a terrific splashing sound made everyone turn and stare behind them.

Swimming very hard across the lake, was a bedraggled, black shape.

'Bledig!' Hester screeched, scrambling down towards the water's edge. ''E must 've 'eard the music and followed the sounds. 'E likes a good tune. Just like me, 'e does!' And her eyes lit up with real happiness.

The figures on the rafts all stood up to see what was happening, craning their necks this way and that. The sudden movements made the rafts rock violently, and most of the dignitaries fell off their carefully placed chairs. Although no one quite fell in, the mayor did drop his speech in the water and, much to everyone's relief, it floated away.

After a few moments, Bledig found that his paws could touch solid rock, and he began to run up the muddy shore. Then, right within range of the lady mayoress' cream silk suit, he stood and shook himself vigorously. The poor woman screamed and fell into her husband's arms. Then they both fell over again, and her huge-brimmed hat, trimmed with pink silk roses, joined her husband's speech, floating away on the river—into the darkest recesses of the chamber.

Limping and bedraggled, Bledig dragged his huge, bony frame up the rocks to his mistress. He sniffed her suspiciously, growling at her and showing the whites of his eyes when she tried to pet him.

'I think he's not used to you having baths, Miss Wookey,' Maddy tried to say tactfully. 'You smell different.'

'So does 'e,' she replied. ''E's 'ad a bath too!'

Bledig sat and looked quizzically at his mistress. Obviously her voice sounded right, even if lavender soap made her smell all wrong. He was frightened and confused. He bared his teeth and growled again.

'I think someone ought to get a vet with a gun,' the manager muttered through gritted teeth. 'Quickly!'

But Hester's ears were very sharp. 'Oi!' she screeched, 'My Bledig ain't going nowhere. No one's going to try and win 'im from me!'

Everyone was puzzled, but Maddy realized that Hester now associated guns with fairground prizes. She leaned as far over the parapet as her plaster cast would allow. She would have to try and explain. 'No Miss Wookey, not that kind of gun. This is one to put Bledig to sleep so he can be got away from all these frightening people. When he wakes up, there'll be a vet, that's an animal doctor, to make sure he's all right and feed him. Then he can come home to you at the flat.'

Hester had been kneeling by Bledig, coaxing him with a gentle voice, trying to get him to recognize her. But a nervous, short, fat figure had come out of the crowd and was standing near Hester, looking rather troubled. 'I'm afraid he won't be able to come to the flat with you, Miss Wookey. He might upset your neighbours.'

Hester and Maddy turned to see who was talking. It was the warden of the flats where Hester lived. She hadn't been able to talk any sense into the old lady over the issue of the window-boxes. However, at the thought of having Bledig chasing all the old dears around the communal gardens, she felt she really *had* to put her foot down this time.

'We have a rule that no one can keep large animals, you see, and Bledig is a *very* large animal indeed. We will have to find a new home for him.' She looked nervously between the huge, black hound and the tough little Hester Wookey.

''E'll calm down,' Hester assured the warden earnestly. ''E'll be good. 'E's just a bit scared an' all. Like I was. 'E'll be all right.'

'I'm afraid a rule is a rule, Miss Wookey.' The warden persisted. She was finding her courage now. 'We'll take him to the RSPCA, and find him somewhere nice, I promise.'

Hester clutched at the protesting, wet dog and shrank back. 'No Bledig, no Hester Wookey! I'm going back in the caves to go to sleep agin. I knew you lot didn't really want me!' And within seconds the poor old lady was crying, heartbroken.

Maddy put out her arm and tried to catch Hester's sleeve as she ran past. 'We do want you, Miss Wookey, and we'd want Bledig too—it's just that he frightens us. And he does growl a lot. Oh dear, I do wish he was small and fluffy and nice like he looked when he was stone…'

And scarcely were the words out of her mouth than there was a soft shower of what felt like rain throughout the chamber and the sound of a bubbling stream… or was it kindly laughter? The water seemed to be blowing on a soft breeze, getting into everyone's eyes and faces. As the guests wiped the water away, and blinked to clear their sight, there came a polite, little yapping from near the floor. There at Hester's feet was a small, bright-eyed Yorkshire terrier, begging to be picked up and cuddled.

For a moment Hester stood, staring, open mouthed. 'Bledig?' she said, incredulous. At the sound of his name, the little animal jumped up again and again, until the old lady bent down and gathered the warm, soft, furry little thing into her arms. The animal licked Hester's face with glee, and she rubbed his fine, silky black hair with delight.

Just then Maddy realized her unplastered leg was wet. She looked down and found her pink coral necklace coiled neatly on her skirt. Then, down below on the raft, Dave jumped from his seat as if something had bitten him. He stood up, grasping something white and wet that had just appeared in his hands. He carefully negotiated the rocking rafts until he came to land, and sprang up the rocks.

He was holding a soggy page from the mayor's speech with writing on the back of it. But not neat, precise copperplate like the wishing wizard used to write, but a gentle, flowing hand with watery, pale blue ink. Dave read it out loud so everyone could hear:

Dear Hester,
Many years ago, when the kind monk from Glastonbury came to see you, he knew you weren't evil, just sad and lonely.
He asked us to help you, because he knew we had

been made to care for the waters and God's creatures underground, just as he had been given the job of caring for those in the open air.

Together we used our skills and powers to hide you in stone so you would be safe from your tormentors. We promised him we would keep an eye on you. Even though you would never speak to us, we always watched you and loved you and cared for you. Now you are free to live your new life, this 'little' Bledig is our gift to you. Think of us sometimes...

The message was not signed, but Hester, Maddy and Dave all knew who it was from—the gentle, kind folk who live in the streams and rivers.

Just then, the manager came bustling up to Hester. 'Everything is in such chaos. Everyone is soaking wet and the mayor's speech has floated away downstream (thank goodness). You had better just unveil the statue, my dear. Then we can all go inside for a hot drink.'

Hester was flustered and nervous. Her cheeks were almost as red as her hat. Shakily, she leaned forward and tugged the long golden cord that ran all the way to the top of the veiled shape beneath the parapet.

As the soft, purple cloth slid down, everyone gasped.

The work was beautiful. At first glance, it was just a lumpy old stalagmite, as Hester had seemed to be for so long, but when one looked closer, there was the face of a thoughtful, wise old woman. The face had been sculpted with strong Saxon bone structure and finely shaped features. The figure sat calm and still, peering out across the cold, green, subterranean lake.

'Funny,' Dave whispered to Tim, 'it's almost alive when you look at it. Yet when you look away and glance back again, it's just a lump of stone once more.'

At the back of the statue was a small brass plate. It was embedded in the rock and had its own special little light so all the passers-by could read it. It said, *'Hester Wookey, the Lady of Wookey Hole.'*

Nick had managed to get to the shore without getting wet. The newspapers wanted him to pose with Hester next to the statue. He put his arm around the old lady and gave her a big, warm kiss on the cheek. 'No one told me you had a dog,' he whispered. 'I hope I'll be allowed to carve a statue of him as well, now.'